Pal Joey

Film Ink Series

★ for copyright reasons these titles are not available in the USA or Canada in the Prion edition.

About the author

John O'Hara (1905-1970) was born in Pottsville, Pennsylvania, the eldest of eight children. He graduated from Niagara Preparatory School, New York State in 1924 and had a succession of jobs – ship steward, gas meter reader, guard in an amusement park, soda fountain assistant – before embarking on his career as a journalist, novelist and short story writer. In much of his fiction Pottsville becomes 'Gibbsville', the setting for his first novel *Appointment in Samarra* (which made him an overnight sensation in 1934) and the backdrop for his explorations of class, social privilege and sexual dynamics. His other works include the notable stage and film successes *Butterfield 8* (1935), *Pal Joey* (1940) and *Ten North Frederick* (1955) for which he received the National Book Award.

PAL JOEY

JOHN O'HARA

This edition published in 1999 by
Prion Books Limited, Imperial Works,
Perren Street, London NW5 3ED

ISBN 1-85375-343-2

Cover design by Jamie Keenan
Cover image courtesy of The Ronald Grant Archive

Printed and bound in Great Britain
by Creative Print & Design, Wales

Contents

introduction

by MATTHEW J BRUCCOLI

John O'Hara (1905-70) published thirteen
novels and twelve volumes of stories. His 400
stories and novellas merit a secure place among
the enduring achievements in American fiction.
During his lifetime O'Hara commanded a loyal
and serious readership in America and Britain:
he enjoyed being congratulated by readers who
recognized him on the streets of London. But
his critical recognition was impeded by his
refusal to advocate fashionable causes and deliv-
er fashionable messages. Critics acknowledged
his "ear for dialogue"—implying that he was
some kind of recording apparatus—while dep-
recating his material and characters. O'Hara was
ignored for twenty-five years after his death,
and his books were allowed to go out of print.
A tardy restoration is now in progress. The only
literary revival that counts is making a writer's
words available.

The *Pal Joey* stories written in 1938-40 had a
strong effect on O'Hara's career. One: they tem-
porarily altered his popular reputation from that
of a chronicler of social history to that of a
show-biz writer. Two: they earned him a great

deal of money from stage and movie musical productions. For a while O'Hara was identified as "the creator of Pal Joey."

John O'Hara provided the genesis of Joey Evans in a 1946 interview with Broadway columnist Earl Wilson: Having "drunk myself sober" at the end of a bender, "remorse set in. I asked, 'What kind of god damn heel am I? I must be worse'n anybody in the world.' Then I figured, 'No, there must be somebody worse than me—but who? Al Capone, maybe. Then I got it—maybe some night club masters of ceremonies I know...That was my idea. I went to work and wrote a piece about a night club heel in the form of a letter." Newspaper gossip columnists are not unnecessarily accurate; yet there must be some truth in this report. The characterization of Joey Evans was initially motivated by O'Hara's antipathy.

The *Pal Joey* stories emulate Ring Lardner's You Know Me Al stories written in the form of letters from a semi-literate baseball player; O'Hara acknowledged his apprenticeship debt to Lardner's dialogue. Lardner's Jack Keefe is a fool and a braggart who elicits the reader's grudging pity; Joey Evans generates dislike combined with a recognition of his self-destructive egoism.

General readers are conditioned to assume that any story written in the vernacular with misspellings is supposed to be humorous. Accordingly, imperceptive readers have tried to find humor in the characterization of Joey

Evans—which is not there. The stories are not funny: they are satirical. Yet many people apparently mistook the Joeys for Damon Runyon's stories about heart-of-gold criminals.

The fourteen *Pal Joey* stories—twelve of which first appeared in *The New Yorker*—were published as a book in 1940 and republished in London in 1952. O'Hara adapted them into the libretto for the 1940 Rodgers and Hart musical, which was regarded as shockingly sexy and ran for 374 Broadway performances; Gene Kelly had his first leading role in this production. Lorenz Hart's witty lyrics ("Bewitched," "I Could Write a Book," "Zip," "Take Him," "Den of Iniquity") perfectly matched O'Hara's raffish material. O'Hara softened Joey's nastiness in the musical. The 1952 Broadway revival had a record run of 540 performances

The 1957 movie version—with which O'Hara was not involved—was rewritten as a vehicle for Frank Sinatra, who was convincing in the role of a womanizing show-business hustler who is not ruthless enough to get his own nightclub. Indeed, the ending indicates that he may be redeemed by the love of the good girl (Kim Novak) after he rejects the possessive rich older woman (Rita Hayworth): "Nobody owns Joey but Joey."

The Joey stories are not among O'Hara's major short stories; series stories tend to become redundant. Even so, they bear the marks of John O'Hara's enduring concern with American social history. He stated in 1960 that

"The United States in the Twentieth Century is what I know, and it is my business to write about it to the best of my ability, with the sometimes special knowledge that I have...I want to record the way people talked and thought and felt, and do it with complete honesty and variety." *Pal Joey* provides a piece of The Master's history of his time: the Thirties entertainment scene of small-time nightclubs, the hotel "Blue Rooms," and the people who worked in them.

Pal Joey

DEAR PAL TED:

Well at last I am getting around to knocking off a line or two to let you know how much I apprisiate it you sending me that wire on opening nite. Dont think because I didnt answer before I didnt apprisiate it because that is far from the case. But I guess you know that because if you knew when I was opening you surely must be aware how busy Ive been ever since opening nite. I figure you read in *Variety* what date I was opening in which case I figure you have seen the write ups since then telling how busy Ive been and believe me its no exagerton.

Well maybe it seems a long time since opening nite and in a way it does to me too. It will only be five weeks this coming Friday but it seems longer considering all that has happened to your old pal Joey. Its hard to believe that under two months ago Joey was strictly from hunger as they say but I was. The last time I saw you (August) remember the panic was on.

I figured things would begin to break a little better around August but no. A couple spots where I figured I would fit in didnt open at all on acct of bankroll trouble and that was why I left town and came out this way. I figured you live in a small town in Michigan and you can stay away from the hot spots because there arent any and that way you save money. I was correct but I sure didnt figure the panic would stay on as long as it did. I finely sold the jalloppy and hocked my diamond ring the minute I heard there would be a chance down this way. I never was in Ohio before but maybe I will never be any place else. At least I like it enough to remain here the remainder of my life but of course if the NBC is listening in Im only kidding.

Well I heard about this spot through a little mouse I got to know up in Michigan. She told me about this spot as it is her home town altho spending her vacation every year in Michigan. I was to a party one nite (private) and they finely got me to sing a few numbers for them and the mouse couldn't take her eyes off me. She sat over in one corner of the room not paying any attention to the dope she was with until finely it got so even he noticed it and began making cracks but loud. I burned but went on singing and playing but he got too loud and I had to stop in the middle of a number and I said right at him if he didnt like it why didnt he

try himself. Perhaps he could do better. The
others at the party got sore at him and told him
to pipe down but that only made him madder
and the others told me to go ahead and not pay
any attenton to him. So I did. Then when I got
finished with a few more numbers I looked
around and the heel wasnt there but the mouse
was. She didnt give me a hand but I could tell
she was more impressed than some that were
beating their paws off. So I went over to her and
told her I was sorry if it embarrassed her me
calling attenton to her dope boyfriend but she
said he wasnt a boyfriend. I said well I figured
that. I said she looked as if she could do better
than him and she said "you for instance" and I
said well yes. We laughed and got along fine and
I took her home. She was staying with her
grandmother and grandfather, two respectible
old married people that lived there all their life.
They were too damn respectible for me. They
watched her like a hawk and one oclock was
the latest she could be out. That to me is the
dumbest way to treat that kind of a mouse. If its
going to happen it can happen before nine
oclock and if it isnt going to happen it isnt
going to no matter if you stay out till nine
oclock the next morning. But whats the use of
being old if you cant be dumb? So anyway Nan
told me about this spot down here and knew
the asst mgr of the hotel where the spot is and

she said she would give me a send in and if I didn't hold them up for too much of the ready she was sure I could get the job. I sing and play every afternoon in the cocktail bar and at night I relieve the band in the ballroom. Anyway I figured I would have to freshen up the old wardrobe so I had to get rid of the jalloppy and hock my diamond ring. I made the trip to Ohio with Nan in her own jalloppy which isnt exactly a jalloppy I might add. Its a 37 Plymouth conv coop. It took us three days to go from Mich. to Ohio but Ill thank you not to ask any questions about my private life.

This asst mgr auditioned me when we finely arrived and I knew right away I was in because he asked me for a couple of old numbers like Everybody Step and Swanee and a Jerry Kern medley and he was a Carmichael fan. Everything he asked me for I gave him and of course I put up a nice appearance being sunburned and a white coat from the proseeds of selling the jalloppy and hocking the ring. I rehearsed with the band altho Collins the leader hates my guts and finely I talked this asst mgr into letting me do a single irregardless of the band and he did.

Well you might say I ran the opening nite. I m.c'd and they had a couple kids from a local dancing school doing tap, one of them not bad altho no serious competition for Ginger Rogers. They were only on for the first week.

They also had another mouse who was with the band, living with the drummer. She tried to be like Maxine. Well she wasnt even colored, thats how much like Maxine she was. The local 400 turned out for the opening nite and inside a week I was besieged with offers to entertain at private parties which I do nearly every Sunday as the bar and ballroom are not open Sunday or at least I do not work. In addition to the job at the hotel and the parties you probably have read about the radio job. I went on sustaining the first week and by the end of the second week I got myself a nice little commercial. I am on just before the local station hooks up with NBC Blue Network five nites a week but I dont think you can catch me in New York. Not yet! My sponsor is the Acme Credit Jewellery Company but I only have eight more weeks to go with them then I am free to negosiate with a better sponsor. Still Im not complaining. Your old pal Joey is doing all right for himself. I get a due bill at the hotel and what they pay me in additon aint hay. I also have the radio spot and the private parties. I went for a second hand Lasalle coop and I am thinking of joining the country club. I go there all the time with some of the local 400 so I figure I might as well join but will wait till I make sure I am going to stay here. I get my picture in the paper and write ups so much that I dont even bother to put them in my scrap book any more. The crowd at the club are always ribbing me about it and accuse me of having the reporters on my payroll but I just tell them no, not the reporters, the editors. I am a little sore at one of the papers because the local Winchell links my name constantly with the name of a very sweet kid that I go to the club and play golf with. Not that it isnt true. We see each other all the time and she comes to the hotel practically every nite with a party and when Im through for the nite we usely take a ride out to a late spot out in the country. Her father is president of the second largest bank. It is the oldest. The biggest bank was formally two banks but they merged. Her name is Jean Spencer and a sweeter kid never lived. I really go for her. But this local Winchell took a personal dislike to me and made a couple cracks about us. One was "That personality boy at a downtown hotel has aired the femme that got him the job and is now trying to move into society." Me trying to move in to society! Society moved in on me is more like it. Jean was burned because she was afraid her father might see the item and when I meet her father I dont want him to have the wrong impression. I think the colyumist got the item from my exfriend Nan. I didnt see much of her when I was rehearsing and the afternoon of opening nite she called up and said she wanted to come but what the hell could I do? Ask for a big table when they were getting $5 a head cover charge? I was glad enough to get the job without asking too many favors. Then a week or so later she called up and asked me could I let her have $50. I asked her what for and she hung up. Well if she didnt even want to do me the curtesy to tell me what for I wasnt going to follow her around begging her to take it. But I gave it a few days thought and decided to let her have it but when I phoned her they said she quit her job and left town. I understand from Schall the asst mgr that she sold her Plymouth and went to N.Y. Her name is Nan Hennessey so if you run into her anywhere youll know her. She could be worse, that is wosse on the eye, a little dumb tho.

Well pally, they will be billing me for stealing all their writing paper if I dont quit this. Just to show you I dont forget I inclose $30. Ill let you have the rest as soon as possible. Any time I can help you out the same way just let me know and you can count on me. I guess you kissed that fifty goodbye but that isnt the way I do things. But I guess you know that, hey pal?

All the best from
PAL JOEY

Ex-Pal

DEAR FRIEND TED:

That is if I can call you friend after the last two weeks for it is a hard thing to do considering. I do not know if you realize what has happen to me oweing to your lack of consideraton. Maybe it is not lack of consideraton. Maybe it is on purpose. Well if it is on purpose all I have to say is maybe you are the one that will be the loser and not me as I was going to do certain things for you but now it does not look like I will be able to do them.

Let us rehearse the whole thing briefley. I wrote to you on the 26 or 7 of last month telling you how I was getting along and inclosing $30 and telling you all the news out here about me getting this radio job and singing in the hotel. Also telling you I was going around with a girl in the local 400 who had a father a banker et cetra. Then I also made the unfortunate error of telling you to look up a certain mouse if you happen to come across her. Which you did and mentioned my name. Well theres the rub. Oweing to your lack of consideraton (mentoning my name) there is hell to pay and I will tell you why. Maybe you know why. Maybe you knew damn well what you were doing and maybe not but anyhow I will tell you just in case.

The way I get it you meet this mouse and right off you shoot off your face about I wrote you and told you to look her up and she gets the wrong impresson because as I understand it she thinks you think all you have to do is menton my name and you are in. Then she gets sore as hell and decides to get even with me. Well here I am 1000 miles from N.Y. and doing OK with my radio job and singing at the hotel and with this kid that has a father a banker and out of the blue everything goes haywire. You knew damn well the mouse I told you about was from this town because I remember distinctly telling you all about her in my letter of the 26 or 7. I remember distinctly telling you she was no tramp and you only drew your own conclusons and not from anything I told you. So here I am doing OK with a car and two good jobs and this society kid going for me and what happens. This is what happens. I do not know what because it is too earley to say.

First of all the asst mgr of the hotel where I am singing he comes to me and says "Joey I just rec'd informaton that is not doing you any good around this town and I want you to level with me and tell me if it is true." What? I said. What informaton? "Well I do not exactly know how to put it man to man. We are both men of the world but this is what I have reference to, meaning that a certain mouse from this town had to leave on acc't of you and is now in N.Y. and instead of helping her you are writing letters to pals in N.Y. and shooting off your face about what a don Juan you are. That dont do you any good personally and I will state frankly that while we are highly pleased with your singing and drawing power as a personality here at the hotel however we have to look at it from all the angels and once it gets around that you are the kind of chap that writes letters to his pals in N.Y. mentoning his fatal attracton to the ladies why some nite some guy is just going to get his load on and you are singing and a guy will walk up and take a poke at you while you are singing. Think it over" he said. Well this asst mgr is a pal of mine and I have the deepest respect for him and I went on & did a couple numbers and after I went to him and got him to tell me all about it. In detail.

So you call yourself a pal. Well that mouse I told you to look up knew this asst mgr in fact I think I told you she introduce me to him. I can see it all clearly. You met her and moved in and then you told her I told you all about her and the little trip we took on the way down from Michigan. As if that wasnt enough the next thing you do you have to destroy the only fine decent thing that has happen to me since coming to this jerk town, namely Jean. Jean is the girl that has a father a banker and it was only a queston of time before I was to meet the family and from there it was only a queston of time before things came to the definitely serious stage, but boy you certanly louse that up. I was to accompany Jean to a private party last Tues. nite and she would pick me up at the hotel after I did a couple numbers and go to this party. Usually when she picks me up she is with another couple but last Tues. when the doorman sent in word she was there she was alone in her Packard conv coop. I thought nothing of it till I notice she was not driving in the directon of this private party and also not opening her trap but just driving and I called her attention to the fact. "No. We are not going to Dwight and Connie Reynolds party this evening" she said. I thought maybe it was called off and said so but she said no it was not called off but she wanted to talk with me. Then out it came. Thanks to you she gets this annonamous letter from that mouse I told you about saying to look out for me that I was a guy that would move in on her and then shoot off my face about it all over. I ask her if I could see the letter and she said she tore it up and I said did she look at the postmark. "Was it postmark N.Y.?" I said. She said no, here, but of course that mouse would send it to some girl friend here and get it postmark here. Well Jean & I had quite a scene much as I dislike scenes and no am't of persuason on my part would convince her it was the work of a lousy bitch that all she was was jealous. "To think that I was on the vurge of inviting you to Sunday dinner next Sunday" she said. That shows how things stood between she & I, but so that is all loused up too.

Well I was frantic. I had come to care deeply for Jean. She lives in a very different world than you and I. Her father is this banker and very conservative and not use to having his daughter going around with chaps that sing in a hotel even if it is one of the principle hotels in the mid west. I go out with all the best people here the 400 but not the older crowd & just on the vurge of going to Jeans house for Sunday dinner she gets this annonamous letter sticking the shiv in my back. Thanks to you. Well I thought for a minute maybe the mouse came home & sent the letter herself and I gave her a buzz Wed. afternoon and a dame's voice answered and when she said who was it I told her and it turned out to be the sister of the one that is causeing all the trouble. When I told her who I was she called me everything she could think of till I thought if anybody was listening in they would think they were overhearing some bag and that she probably is because you got to be a bag to know some of the things she called me.

She also made threats and said one of these nites she was coming down to the hotel when I was doing a number and would personally spit in my eye and knock me the hell off the stand. Then I told her what I thought of her *and* her sister and if she ever showed her face around the hotel I would knock her teeth down her throat. Woman or no woman. I shut her up the bitch. I said she and her fine feathered sister. Well I said if she wanted to know anything about her sister ask anybody that was in Michigan last summer and she would find out what I meant. So if you see the mouse again you can tell her. I dont give a damn if I lose my job here at the hotel or the radio spot. I dont have to take that stuff from any mouse or her sister. As for you my ex-pal you know what you can do and also you can sing for the $20 I owe you. I am making a little trip to N.Y. in the near future and we will have a little talk and you can explain your positon, altho the way I feel now if I saw you now your positon would be horizontle. I might as well tell you I am going to the gym 3 or 4 times a week and not that I need it because I always could slap you around when ever I wanted to.

> You know what you can do.
> YOUR EX-PAL JOEY

How I am Now in Chi

PAL TED:

Well, pally, I have come to the concluson that old pals are best and never put too much faith in new acquaintances or you will end up two away from the 9 ball. When I tell you that you are getting it straight from head–quarters, because I know. I have been thinking it over and the true test of friendship is if you can weather such things as for instance you and I, meaning like differences of opinon over a mouse or the dough department and things on that order. You and I certainly have had our differences of opinon over the above yet here I am when I think it over and give the matter mature consideraton I think of you as a friend and I always hope you will consider me a friend if you have the ill fortune of ever getting in a spot in which I found myself recently. Then you can count on me altho' hoping the occason does not arise. (God forbid.)

Well I recall telling you about a little mouse one of the local 400 that her father was president of the bank (largest in town). This mouse Jean

by name use to come every night to the hotel
to hear me sing and it got so it was embarrass-
ing owing to the fact that those lugs in the band
would begin to kid me about it. They would
say that mouse has got it for Joey but bad. She
would come there and sit and just look at me
and when she would get up to dance and I
would sing and she would just stand there in
front of me with her escort and it became so
that it was obvious and altho' I pride myself on
being equal to such situatons (having had the
experience before) it use to disconcert me more
than I can say. However she arranged an introduction and I use to take her out especially
when I was singing at private parties of the local
400. In a short time she use to stop for me at
the hotel damn near every evening and I came
to care for her as she was different than the
usual ones that make a fool of themselves over
a singer or entertainer. We were reaching the
stage where it was you might say only a queston
of time before Joey and Jean would veil up and
perhaps I would consider giving up this life.
Not that I ever intended doing that but she use
to discuss it with me. She often use to ask me if
I thought my life interesting and was it fun and
how did I happen to get in it and of course that
was her subtile way of getting me to consider
probably going into the banking game with her
father after we got married.

Well of course she was ninteen years old and one for the book as far as looks, figure, personality is concerned and also had plenty of scratch, being the bank presidents daughter. I went to work and bought a couple new arrangements in fact she gave me one for Xmas last Xmas. I happen to say one night I needed a couple new arrangements and she asked me how much they were and I told her my guy charged $50. She also gave me a set of studs and cuff links to wear with my tails that must have set her back the price of four arrangements. It was her favorite song at the time, the arrangement she gave me. It was You go to my Head. I had an old arrangement of it from last summer but never had any call for it but she use to like it before she met me and so I got out the old arrangement and of course did not spoil it for her by saying it was one I had last summer and never had any call for. However I used the 50 to give her a Xmas present, a sport watch.

Then around the end of January they were having this ball in honor of the President (Roosevelt) to get up a fund that they would give for this infantile paralasys. Very white of them as they sit around all year and say what a heel he is and on his birthday they give him this ball and it is a club called the Junior League that she belonged to had charge of getting the talent and all that like publicity etc. So of course I

gladly donated my services as I was going anyway having planned to escort Jean to the ball.
The ball was in the ballroom of the hotel but I
was going to escort her from her house. Then at
the very last minute I said to her what should
we do that evening until it was time to go to
the ball (11:30 or 12) and she said she was going
to a dinner party at these friends of hers named
Fenton. I said it was a fine time to tell me that
and said I consider it a fine thing to go to the
Fenton's for dinner knowing that they were one
of the few that took a snobbish attitude in con-
nection with me. I told her she could take it or
leave it and if she went to their house for dinner she could count me out on the subject of
escorting her to the ball. I was plenty burned
and she said she never understood I was taking
her anyway and of course she was right. I took
it for granted and didnt bother to ask her until
the last minute and then I said well I will just
stop for you at the Fenton's about 11:30 and
that will save you the trouble of coming to the
ball alone or with another couple. Imagine my
surprise to learn that she already had an escort,
Jerry Towle a young dope that does nothing but
fly his own plane and scaring farmer's horses
and always in some kind of a jam with the law
but his old man has plenty of scratch and gets
him out of it. I said you go with Towle and let
him take you every other place from now on

and I said and dont bother to come to the hotel any more but stay away and our date for the next night was off.

Well we had a quarrel about that and it ended up I didn't go to the Fenton's and when I was singing that night at the ball she made Towle dance her up and request Go to my Head but I said very politely I only had the newer numbers and did not sing Go to my Head this year. Did she burn? I didn't even dance with her and I only sat with the boys in the band all night and then went up to my room after I did my numbers and called up some hustler and took her to a hamburger joint where the 400 go every night after dances and hoped Jean and Towle would come in but they never did so I gave the hustler 5 bucks for her time and sent her home in a taxi.

Well the next night I am singing and in she comes but I never give her a tumble but she gets her load on I notice and about one a.m. a note comes over by waiter and she wants me to meet her but she is with this party and I am burned so I dont answer the note. I just tell the waiter no reply and when I finish my last number I screw and go around the corner to have a cup of coffee and there she is, followed me. I do not want to make a scene then and there and she has her load on and will not go back and rejoin her party so I send around and get my car out of the garage hoping to take her for a ride and sober her up but oh no. Instead we go for a ride and altho' it was freezing and we did not have a coat either of us we are out for about an hour and always fighting and it began to get late and I knew the grill at the hotel would be putting the chairs up on the tables so I ignored her and turned around and went back. No sign of her party. They have gone. That means I have to take her home and she lives out in the suburbs and by the time we get there somebody has called her up to see if she got home and woke up the old man and he is waiting for her in a dressing gown. She is still plastered the little lush and her old man asks what the meaning of this is and who am I and bringing his daughter home in this condition. Then I tell him who I am and he says Oh, he has heard about me and has always wanted to meet me and without any warning brings one up from the floor and I stop it with my chin, as dirty a punch as I ever saw. I got up but had the presence of mind so that I did not let him have one but said I dont want any part of his daughter, the lush. Keep her home or he would be a grandfather one of these days without a son in law. I think he would have got a gun but I was out of there before he had the chance.

Well the next a.m. about 10 the phone rings and it is the manager, my boss. He wants me

down in his office so I go and he hears all about
it only an exageraton of what really happened.
To make a long story short I am out. I say what
about my contract and he says read your contract and then I remember he had the right to
fire me if I get out of line and he gives me the
rest of the week (pay) and an extra week and
says he advised me to lam out of there as I
insulted the most powerful man in the whole
town as I will soon find out. I find out alright.
I call up this ad agency that pays me for singing
on the local radio staton where my sponsor is
this credit jewelry company. They were just
about to call me. I am out. The mouse's old
man only owns the God damn staton. I go to a
lawyer but he wont take my case as he says I
havent any case. Even if I had he would think
twice about bucking this mouse's old man. So
there I am holding an empty bag with my
wardrobe and a car only about half paid for and
all told about a little over 300 in my kick. So I
go back to the hotel and start in packing (about
5 in the afternoon this is) and a messenger
comes and brings me a note from Jean. She is
sorry about it and did not want to cause me all
this trouble and would do anything to make or
mend. Her old man had her at the doctor's or
she would have got in touch with me sooner
and will I call her at this number, a girl friend
of hers. They are going to take her to some

place in N. Carolina the next day and she has to
see me. I do not have to worry as the dr. says she
is okay, but she would not be able to stand it
going away like this with me feeling this way all
over a little thing like a misunderstanding over
the Fenton's dinner and she heard her old man
threaten to get me bounced out of town etc
and she is desperate because she loves me. Well
I thought it over and what a fine chance I had
to show her old man who was the most powerful man in town as far as his own family are
concerned. All I had to do was pick up Jean and
drive over the state line and inside of two hours
he would have a son in law alright. I am sitting
there debating within myself as to whether I
will call her or not and the door opens. "You
know me," he says. Towle. "I see you are packing.
Good. There is a 9 oclock for Chicago and an
8.30 for N.Y. and I would suggest the 8.30 but
I leave the choice entirely up to you," he says. "I
think I will sit around and take you to the
train." I ignore him but go on packing and when
I finish up I send down and have room service
bring me up a steak sandwich with French fries,
a cup of coffee and a piece of pie and I eat it
there with him sitting there. I had to pay cash
for it as room service will not let me sign. Then
I lit a butt and smoke it calmly and then I phone
the railroad and order a lower on the 9 oclock
for Chi. I can see he is burned but that is what

I intend. Then the phone rings and he answers it and says he is not here but has just left and then he says "Dont be a damn fool Jean this is Jerry and yes he is here but you are not going to see him if I can help it and you may not speak to him as I am acting on your fathers orders." Then he hangs up. He is a big lug. Over 200.

Well I phone the garage and tell them to put my car into dead storage and take out the battry and then it is time to go to the train and he goes with me. When we get there I tell him he can have the pleasure of paying the taxi and he says it is a pleasure alright and I said I thought it would be and also a pleasure for me. When I go to get my ticket he even pays for the ticket, tips the porter, etc. I did not lose my sense of humor. I said "By the way I have nothing to read on the train" and he buys me papers and magazines. I see the humor in it and I also say I always have chewing-gum on trains so he buys me some gum. But he does not see the humor for when the train is ready to pull out I reach out my hand and say it was a pleasure to have him come down and see me off, him of all people, and just then he hauls off and slaps my hand, burned like I never saw anybody burned.

Well the train pulled out and that is the story of how I am now in Chi. I am singing for coffee & cakes at a crib on Cottage Grove Ave. here. It isn't much of a spot but they say it is lucky as four or five singers and musicians who worked here went from here to big things and I am hoping. Well give my best to Artie and Fred and Chink and Mort. Tell Mort congratulations as I hear he is starting up a new band and I would be willing to work for scale. Tell Fred when he comes out to look me up as I plug his last two numbers every nite. Well Ted all the best and I don't have to say I think your solo in Jeepers Creepers is as good as Vanuti. I am glad a pal is having such good luck and I mean that sincerely as ever. Will write soon again.

PAL JOEY

Bow Wow

Dear Friend Ted:

Well pal I had to sit down the minute I came home just returning from a furniture store around the corner from where I am living. Having just heard what you did to Hong Kong Blues. Well if I was ever proud of a friend I am proud of you alright. To say it is a wonderful recording is to say the least. I happen to drop in at this store as I do every week to hear the new recordings. You know me, Ted. Strictly larceny when it comes to listening to those arrangements but I cant afford to buy any new arrangements of my own right now so I have to get them from recordings and take the best of this one and that one. The joint where I am singing and m. c-ing in is satisfied with my work and it keeps me in coffee & cakes but not much more. As a pal of mine said the other night Chicago is alright if you like Chicago altho I would rather be back in N.Y. or even go to Frisco for the other Fair. I have had one or two propositons in regards to Frisco but nothing attractive. That is to make it worth while going all the way out there and then maybe getting stuck where I dont know anybody. I dont know what to do so for the moment am sticking here getting my coffee & cakes and building up a local following. They have a place out on the North side that has made me one or two offers but I will stay down in this territory until I get a propositon from some place in the Loop dist. I figure I ought to go good in a place like the Chez Paris, tops here, or maybe one of the hotels. Downey always goes good here altho his stuff is of course different than mine. Well enough of my problems. I only wanted to conveigh my congratulatons on the new recordings and for a young band. Who have you got on the guitar? If I didnt know McDonough was dead I would say it was him. I also thought I recognized Fud but I guess he is still with Tommy so guess I am an error.

Well I guess you wonder what I do with my spare moments out in this bailwick. Write letters is one thing. Just think a year ago you were the one crying the blues and less than a year ago I was doing alright with the Packard etc. And now you are up there and there will be no stopping you and believe me you have the ardent wishes of success from all your pals. I am getting by in this crib in Chi. but guess I have learned my lesson and am a changed man. All because of a dog.

Well this is the first time I wrote since I bo't
Skippy the name of my dog and it is wonderful
what they can do. They give you the courge to
continue when things look bad. I use to hear Al
White on the subject of man's best friend the
dog and use to laugh myself sick when White
would rib the love and affecton of a man and a
dog but he is wrong. There is something to it.
It worked in my case as when I came out here
I didnt have any job and took the first thing that
came along and took the attitude that the world
was a pretty sorry place to live in and it effected
my work. I would get up to do a number and
took the attitude that I hated all the people
there and I guess it showed because Lang (no
relaton to Eddie) the owner of this spot gave
me a call. He said get more of a pleasing personality in it or pack. It put the fear of God in
me as I wasnt there long enough to build up a
following and had not stashed any dough away.
Also no prospects or propositons from other
spots and of course this joint dont spend any
dough advertising and the press agent gets no
pay but only a certan am't of drinks on the cuff
so you can imagine how hard he works. So I
gave the matter my mature consideraton and
then that week I was out getting my breakfast
around 4 one afternoon and right near where
I eat is this pet & dog shop. I never had any
interest in dogs and never considered owning

one and thought they were a nusaince especially in towns. But I saw this mouse standing there
bent over and talking to one of the dogs in the
window of the shop. She was about twenty and
I didnt care if she had a face out of the Zoo but
spring was in the air and this mouse had a shape
that you dont see only on the second Tuesday of
every week and when you do see a shape like
that you have to do something about it. So I
stopped and feined an interest in the dog king-
dom and cased the mouse and got a look at her
kisser. Well it fitted in with the rest of the body.
Not pretty but cute. She had personality in her
face I could see that. She didnt see me because
she was so crazy about this one dog that had his
nose up against the window and she was talking
to it before she noticed me and then got sort of
embarassed when she saw me. But by that time
I was looking at the dog and smiling at him and
leaned over and started talking and the first
name I could think of came to my head and I
said hello Skippy boy. And the mouse looked at
me and said is that his name, Skippy? I said I
didnt know I only pretend it was. I said I pass
by here every day and got to love him so much
that I had to give him a name like the name of
an airdale dog I used to have when I was a kid.
Oh so I love dogs, she wanted to know and I
said yes. Then she said why didnt I buy this
puppy and I said for the same reason why I

didn't buy a Dusenburg, money. Well the effect
it had on her was wonderful. I could see tears in
her eyes and she said it was a shame that anybody that love dogs so much had to be deprived
of them because of the finances where so many
people that didnt really love them had them and
didnt treat them properly. Yes, I said, that is true.
I said I was saving up so I could buy Skippy and
there was a sign in the window that said $30.
That part was the truth, that is, I didn't have any
$30 to buy any dogs with. I began telling her
about Skippy the airdale that I didnt have when
I was a kid and pretty soon got to believing it
myself, all about how my heart was broken
when poor little Skippy was crushed beneath
the wheels of a 10 ton truck. I said my family
were well to do people in those days and
wished to buy me another dog but I said to
them no dog would take the place of Skippy
and never would until one day I happen to be
going by this shop and my eye caught this little
puppy's and something about him reminded me
of Skippy and she said yes, he was a little like an
airdale. Well I didnt know an airdale from a hole
in the ground and didnt know what the hell
this mut was in the window and so I said it
wasnt the breed, I said, it was just something in
this puppy's expresson that reminded me of my
old Skippy. She was touched. She said she never
would of taken me for somebody that loved

dogs so much and I said you dont know much about dogs then, Miss. I said dogs have strange tastes in people and only a dog knows who he likes. By this time Skippy was laying down and I said he is tired and I said I had to go and get my breakfast. I said this is the only time of the day that I can see Skippy as they take them out of the window soon. Just a guess but I didnt seem to remember seeing the dogs in the window late in the afternoon and the mouse said "Did I hear correctly when you said you were going to have breakfast?" And I said yes, I am one of those unusual people that their days are upside down. I said you are probably the kind that would be having tea now but I am having breakfast. That made her laugh and so I took advantage of that and said why not have tea with me if she didnt mind sitting at a counter for it? As I said before I had cased this mouse and she was pretty but I knew she was no society debutante. Probably a stenog out of work but very cute. So she said she often ate at counters and went with me. I was right and she was a stenog looking for work. She went with me to this one-arm where I eat and she had a tomato on rye and a coffee and I had eggs and coffee and we started talking and it turned out she was from some little town in Illinois, not Peoria but some place like it. Her name was Betty Hardiman and lived with her married sis-

ter and her husband and only came to Chi a
month before. I told her my people lost all their
money in the crash and I had to leave Princeton
college and go to work but the only work I was
suited for was singing with a band or in a night
club and then she said she recognized my name
from passing the club on her way to the L. She
said she thought people that worked in clubs
got plenty of money and I said it depends on
what club and then when it came time to pay
the check she said she would pay her own and
insisted and said let me consider that her con-
tributon to buying Skippy.

Well I said I hoped she would come around
to the club some time with her boy friend and
I would sing any number she would request and
she said her boy friend didn't live in Chi but
went to college at the Illinois U. at Champaign.
I said well she should come some time with her
sister and her husband and Betty said her bro.
in-law never went to night clubs and I said I
guess it was pretty dreary for a young girl living
like that and she said it was becoming that way
altho it was better than home. She said she
loved Chi, just going around the Loop and
watching the people's faces on the L trains, but
would like to see some more of the fun but her
boy friend was working his way thru the Illinois
U. and didnt get to Chi only two or three times
a year. Well I said this is very pleasant but I had

to go and rehearse a couple numbers at the club and got her phone number and said I would like to take her out some night if I got a night off and she said she tho't it would be alright.

Well I saw her a couple times but only in the day time. We use to meet at the dog shop. We would go to the one-arm and then I would have to leave her but one afternoon she borrowed her bro. in-law's car and drove out to the country and I gave her a little going over but not too much as I could tell the time was not ripe. I was even surprised I could neck her at all on acc't of this boy friend at the Illinois U., but I guess it was the first time a pass was made at her since the last time she saw the college boy and I guess she needed a little work-out. Well that night I hit a crap game for about eighty clams and two days later I met Betty and told her and she said now I could buy Skippy and I said no, unfortunately the flea-bag where I was living did not permit dogs. I said that was just my luck. Then I said I have an idea. I said how about if I buy him for her and she could keep him and on conditon that she would let me see him and she said she would love to but would have to ask her sister as they only had an apartment. I met the sister by that time and I knew she went for me but had not met the bro. in-law. She asked the sister but the sister said no. Betty couldn't have a dog in the ap't because it was too small, much as she would love to have a dog. So then I went to my landlady and asked her if I could have a dog and she said sure so then I went to Betty and told her I had a deal with my landlady that if I paid more rent I could keep the dog so Betty was overjoyed and I bo't Skippy. The landlady has a kid about ten or eleven and he takes care of Skippy for me. Takes him for his walks and washes him and the landlady thinks I am a fine young fellow but why shouldnt she when her kid has the use of a $30 dog for nothing. I often have fun with the mut too and pat him and I often think if it wasn't for Skippy I never would of met Betty. Her sister and bro. in-law are going away the week-end after next and we will have the ap't all to ourselves. It's about time but I had to be patient as she said she wanted to be sure first, but a man with such a love and affecton for dogs was a man you could trust. Well, pal, all the best and keep your eyes open for any spots you hear for me. I would rather be around N.Y. this summer as it gets hot as hell out here in summer but if you hear anything like a good spot with a band touring or some summer hotel in Mass. or Maine dont forget your pal. I have no contract here as they never heard of a contract at a crib like this so can leave at a moment's notice. Of course it will be worth sticking around a month or so if you get what I mean. Bow wow.

PAL JOEY

Avast and Belay

FRIEND TED:

Well, chum, still in Chi, doing alright and have my notices to prove it like one critic that I hardly know at all that works on a throwaway that they distribute at hotels etc. but is far the best writer in the nite life and he goes on to say I am the smoothest and most urbane singer of sophisticated melodies this town has seen in many a moon, and it was not a case of me taking an ad to get the write-up as the 1st I knew of it was when somebody showed it to me. "What is he your cousin?" said one of the lightweights in the band as he ignore the band and just gave them a menton in passing and devoted all his write-up to me. I only menton this now because I have in mind an idea that I want to discuss with you in this letter.

Well, chum, this is the idea I have been taking under consideraton and the pro's & con's ever since around the beginning of Sept. but more so lately owing to a conversaton I had with another chap recently. You would not know the name

if I told you but his name is Charley Goas.
Charley is a man around 40 odd yrs of age and
a mind like a steel trap and knows all the angles.
He is still alive today but use to be a big
accountaint for Capone or one of the big mobs
out here like Capone or perhaps it was Bugs
Moran or Deeny O'bannon or Collosimo. I
never asked him that as he was not a mob guy
himself but just did their accountaincy for them
and I would not know that only I happen to ask
somebody what he did and they told me. I
think he owns a piece of the room where I sing
in now but I am not suppose to know that and
do not pipe. Well he took a liking to me and
drops in every nite and we struck up an acquan-
tainceship and I guess he more or less considers
me like a kid bro. as he often gives me advice
like on more than 1 occason he saw me looking at a mouse and when I looked at him he
smiled and without me saying anything he said
to me, "That's for you, eh? O.K. sonny boy if
you want to end up on crutches." So that shows
how he took an interest in me and I apprisiate
it and therefore when he offered me some other
advise I also took it or am starting to take it by
giving you this idea I have in my mind.

This is the set-up. Charley was telling me one
nite how it looked like a sure thing there was
going to be a war. Next day, they declare war,
and there was a rumor around that the room

would fold because business stank but I happen to know that Charley told the backers they shouldnt be silly. They were ahead enough so they could take a few bad nites and if business didnt pick up why then fold but dont fold until they saw if business was going to stay stinking or perhaps get better. Charley was right. We kept open and business is better than ever.

So all during this I got a chance to talk to Charley about the war and he got to remenissing about in the last war. I do not know for a fact if he was in the army or navy as with Charley you leave Charley do the talking and never ask questions. However he asked me what my plans were and I said I did not give it much tho't as I did not think we would be in it and time enough when we got in. "Dont be silly," said Charley. "We will be in it before the horses stop running at Hialeah." This came as rather a surprise to me but before I had the opportunity to discuss it with him he said pick your spots now and do not be a sucker and get drafted. Then they can put you where they want to but if you pick yr. spot now you can stay in it and he said "Not this bunch of plumbers but do you have a contact with a guy with a good band" and I said "yes" and mentoned you as one of my eldest friends and he said he heard of you and said flattering things about you on the air and said he never met you but caught you & the band somewhere and got the impresson you have a wonderful personality and I agreed with him extremely. Well he said I was a fool if I did not make some kind of a propositon with you like get you to join the navy. Wait a minute now and read it all before you think I am going wacky. He said if a jig band by the name of Jim Europe (probably his professional name) during 1917 could be a big success in Paris why not a fellow like you, a name band known from coast to coast on the air and by records. He said there was this jig name Jim Europe had a band and they just about ran Paris in the war and after it until somebody took a shot at Mr. Europe and that ended him. All those Parisienns went for the band too which is a handy thing in a war. Acc. to Charley they even made this jig a liu-tenant in the U.S.A. and he was a regular offi-cer with a snappy uniform and white guys had to salute him owing to him being an officer. Well if they did that they ought to do it for you. He said take for instant Sousa, John Phillips Sousa and I remember him, the march king. My old lady used to never tire of Sousa on the phonograph until in desperaton I broke the damn records and my old man belted me for it as he also use to listen to them altho he did not know a note of music but was a son of a bitch for finding the nearest bar if you pardon the gag. Well Sousa had this big corny band all brass and what did they do but make him a kind of an admiral. Stars & Stripes For-ever and Shine Little Glow-worm was the kind of stuff he played so you can write your own ticket with your repretory. He didn't play good but played loud and so my 1st suggeston is get more brass and gradually expand the size of the band and if I were you I would give the boot to that rum-pot you have now and get yourself a real press agent that could get yr. picture in the Life mag-azine and maybe it would be a good idea to get navy uniforms and also get up a few routines like Waring use to have. Drills, only learn to march instead of those routines with cocktail shakers etc. that Waring use to have. All this is my idea not Charley's as he only contributed the original tho't and I put my brain to work on what you could do if I called yr. attenton to it.

I am not trying to tell you how to run yr. band as you do alright without me and once in a while when I tho't to myself Ted ought to do this or that I refrained from telling you as it is your band not mine. However this war stuff is an angle you may not of thought of.

I am only scratching the surface with these suggestons and have many more that are on the same order but better and these randam notes now are just suggestons or hints but ought to get yr. mind running in that directon. We could do big things and at the same time be patriotic doing it. As I understand it we ought to figure on just the regular pay which is of course naturally way below scale as when you are working for Uncle Sam he never heard of scale but would pay $30 a month to the ones with the rank of private and only cigarette money to a leader like yourself but of course I guess it would be understood with the army or navy that you could do jobs and records and of course a big patriotic band would get all the cream if you start soon enough. I have a slogan "put your band on the bandwagon" before the others get hep. I say we all the time because I take for granted you would get me a pardon out of this joint Chicago if you decide I have a good idea. If you wanted to put me on the payroll now I could give this joint notice just by saying why dont you guys go take a flying etc. and take a powder out of here that day and be in N.Y. the next. A wire will do the trick Ted boy. I will level with you. I get an honest yard here and was only saying that for laughs when I told you I got $150 the way we all exagerate in this business. You could go on working while I talk to the Army and Navy guys and whichever offers us the best propositon you can be sure I will take that one. Then when war is declared we are in uniform and ready to go that nite. Maybe by that time you would consider me such a good mgr. that you would have me for your peace-time mgr. even before we get in the war. I would find out in advance (from Charley) when we are getting in the war and would book you into some big Bway spot in time so that nite when war is declared we would be there in our uniforms. Think of the flash, as they use to say in vaudeville days. The 1st Swing Band in Uniform! It would be plastered all over the papers and with the right handling I see you shaking hands with the President at the White House, him congratulating you for being the 1st band in kahki, altho I hope the navy give us the better propositon as for a band the navy has better toggery.

Well think it over Ted because Charley says the time is getting short. Charley says before the hay-burners stop running at Hialeah. John Phillips Sousa was an old man so they had to make him an admiral but admiral sounds too old for you so if we decide the navy offers us the better propositon you could be a Commander. I could be a Leutenant Commander. One thing I will add to the informaton above which is this. I am only kidding about telling these Chicago guys where to head in and this is why. It is because Charley says during the last war they had anywhere from 10 to 50,000 sailors in Chi. believe it or not. They had a training camp here for sailors and that was as close as they got to getting their head shot off.

If they got their head shot off it would be in a crap game amongst themselves or in a riding academy on the South Side. I am more in favor of the navy but of course will take the better propositon. "So get the band aboard the band-wagon" Ted and I am ready the moment you give the downbeat. Charley said a band like this no doubt would be booked for liberty bond engagements when they start selling liberty bonds to the people. I tho't of an angle there and asked Charley "Suppose we are booked into a town to sell these liberty bonds for the government do we get our per-cent. of the gross" but Charley said not with Mr. Whiskers at the gate, nobody cuts in on Mr. Whiskers. But it just shows I was looking out for our interest. Also Charley may be wrong. He can be. He thinks his wife doesnt like me and boy he is so wrong.

Well Commander, avast and belay and all that sort of thing.

Your pal
JOEY

P.S.: I also want to warn you Vallee was in the navy in the last war and may have a good in there so we have to work fast so he wont crab our act.

Joey on Herta

DEAR PAL TED:

Well Pal I suppose you did not hear that yrs. truly the undersigned and to-wit has manage to build up a following so that they are borrowing the money wherewith to enlarge the joint and take care of the bigger and higher class clintele which followed on the heels of when I put over "Waiter with the Water"? But it is good news that you are banging them right over every where you go. I hear nothing but the best reports of you and the band and it is no secret that when you played the Palomar in Los Angeles, for a fairly recent band you broke the house record. Maybe you did not break the Goodman or Artie Shaw record but they made their record with an establish band and of course you went in there with scarcely if any radio build-up and still did terrific business. I am sure you glorify in your success and believe me when I say nothing could make me happier than you being right up there where you belong and am sure will not change in regard to your old pals. Might like to know later developments on how I am doing. Well here goes.

I told you the details and how I got creamed out of the hotel spot in Ohio & came here and made this connecton. For a while I was from hunger but suddenly clicked as it were over night. With me it was one of those things, just one of those crazy things. One nite singing a lung out for dopes that wouldn't know it if I was Toscanini, Al Rinker, or Brooks John or myself. All they cared about was if I sang Deep Purple 75 times a nite and they were satisfied. Female lushes that they would stand right under me while their escorts were giving them a little going over and I and the band were not suppose to see it. Oh no, just dumb, is what we were. I use to stand up there giving them Deep Purple and all the time the tho't kept cropping up in my mind "I only wish I had a water pistol, an old fashon water pistol such as we played with as a child and wouldn't I like to squirt you right in the eye with it Madam right in the mist of your memory Madam." But one nite I happen to get a small slice of Phil Harris broadcasting from Los Angeles and happen to tune in when he was polishing off Hold Tight. I said this can not be the guy that formerly I use to consider a road company Richman but it was. I knew there would be no trouble at all so I polished off his Hold Tight and practicly over nite I was the

one man attracton of this joint. Then I caught
Harris again one nite doing Fishes and from
then on I and the joint were but set. The owner
(only fronting for one of the many mobs they
still got left here in Chi) gave me a quick hist in
pay and began to talking contract but no said I.
No contract now. Let's wait? (Meaning maybe
some advertising agency might grab me off and
did not want to be stuck with any contract.) So
I let on like I was very happy at this joint & the
only reason I was saying no contract was
because I was coresponding with my agent in
N.Y. and my hands were tied until hearing from
him. That is a laugh, my agent. After they tied a
can to my tail in Ohio there wasn't an agent in
the U.S. that would give me a tumble. However
that is neither here nor there but is a sample. So
they put my name outside in lights and I was in
but good.

Well I started out to tell you a little experence
I had which just goes to show you how the
leaches fasten upon a person practicly before they
have time to turn on the lights that spell out his
name. This one nite after I began clicking there
was this large party given by a bowling club
consisting of people in the neighborhood that
belong to this neighborhood bowling club and
met some nite every wk. in order to indulge
themselves in their silly pastime and this nite
was the nite when they had their annual get-

together for the purpose of the distributon of
the awards & prizes and of course they had
about 40 or more there, men & women. Well
the press agent of this joint said to me it would
make a nice gesture if I would make a few reference to this club when I introduced my numbers and dedicate some numbers to them. He
kept talking about cagling. The only Cagle I
ever heard of was a football player that use to
play for West Point years ago but Cagling is also
the name for bowling so I made a few wise
cracks about Cagling that the p. a. gave me and
I also put one of my own in about Keg-lined
beer cans altho why I should give a plug to
Bernie's ex-sponsor I do not know only that it
occurred to me at the time. It went over big and
they liked me and soon were standing around
asking for request no's.

I happen to notice in the sea of faces this one
kisser that stood out in the crowd. About 21
and naturally blonde hair and complected and
most likely a Swede I tho't. So then when they
all insisted that I join them I naturally obliged
them and this mouse named Herta Gersdorf
was the one I gradually sat next to. One word
led to another and it turned out she would like
to be a singer and so to make a nice gesture to
the club and for good will etc. I said I have an
announcement to make and Miss Herta Gersdorf will sing. She pretend to be surprised but

did not fool me as I knew she was working on me to do that very thing, so I brought her up to the mike and asked her what she wanted to sing and what key but she did not know what key, only the name of the song. Three guesses. Day in Day Out. I encouraged her and got her started and to my amazement she turned out to have a voice not of course a trained voice and had no experence in singing in public but I detected possibilities in the voice and began to think to myself I had a find. Well she got a big hand of course being a member of the cagle club and they did not detect the rough edges and amateur touches or if they did they forgave her owing to her youth and lack of experence singing in public. So I helped her with an encore and of course I made a lot of friends for the joint and also increased my own following by the gesture. Well I talked to her and inquired did she ever consider doing it professionally (singing I mean) and she said she always use to dream of it but knew there was no chance. So I said I would gladly help her and got her phone no. and she said she would have to ask her parents and the next day or 2 days later she called me up and said they would like it if she could take lessons from me but could not afford to pay anything and I said that would be o.k. So for a week I went to her house every nite when she got home from stenogging in the real estate

office where she worked and showed her a few
things then after the 1st wk. I brought her to
the joint and late every afternoon I would show
her some mike technique and the difference
between singing in front of a mike & without
it. She was a dumb little mouse but willing to
learn. So all the time I was thinking this was
going to be my favorite dish but at the time did
not do anything about it as I was being taken
care of but too good by a dame that had a little
dress shop in the neighborhood. Anyway I
never made a pitch with Herta. I was afraid it
would Herta. So what I did was find out she
was 21 and looked up an old agreement I had
with an agent the 1st time I ever had an agent
and copied it down and she signed it making
me her agent in case she clicked. Therefore I
went to the "owner" of the joint and said I had
this mouse and told him she was popular and
had a voice which I was training and of course
the 1st thing that heel did was he said he wanted to warn me to watch my step and don't get
any bad reputaton in the neighborhood kids or
there would be hell to pay and the patrons
would stop coming in imagine! I said to him he
could let me worry about my conduct, morals,
etc. and he said Oh if there was any worrying to
do I better do it which sounded pretty sinistre
but he was not throwing any scare into me for
I replied to him let us pass over that phase of it

and get down to business, did he or did he not
want this mouse she being under contract to
me in a strictly business legitamite deal and
showed him the contract. I said acting as artists
representative for the girl I wanted $35 a wk.
for her services and we dickered until he came
up to 25 and then I said its a deal so I swung the
job for her. It was about time something like
that happen to me after all the hard luck I been
having and also it was about time Herta was
getting around to paying something on acc't as
she never paid me a nickel for my instructon
and lessons and rehearsals and my time, etc, and
her parents never offer to pay anything either so
it was a lucky thing for her I got her the job as
it enabled her to pay me back $25 a wk. for the
instructon & time and lessons etc. and I was able
to continue giving her lessons while she
worked. I shamed her mother into getting up
$30 for an evening dress. I took one look at the
dress they picked out for her and said to them
"May I inquire if you think Herta is singing for
a choir?" I did not want to lose my temper
therefore the gag. The kid was built on the
order of Babs whatever her name was that
worked with the band when you use to play
horn with Joe and here they were trying to
make her wear a dress for a convent of sisters.
So I entered into the situaton and informed
them that I would take care of the clothes dept.

and out of my own pocket advanced her $9.50 so she could pour herself into a $39.50 no. that showed everything but her scar where she had the appendisetis if she ever had it (some spelling I admit). Also advanced her $5 to get her hair fixed up and fingernails etc. Well I put her over but big and she only fumbled one no. a little and I tho't at the time after the 1st nite she was going to be grateful as she seemed grateful at the time. I was of course going on with the instructon etc. and let her have for nothing a couple arrangements I was thinking of polishing off for myself. Also featured her in my own duets and also gave her a small break when I would introduce her nos. I would introduce her as my protege Herta. (I dropped her last name but only used Herta like Hildegard the singer that doesn't say her last name either because it is some name from Milwaukee or some place.) It went over. But little did I know.

Low & behold one nite before she went on she said to me she had to be good that nite because her boss & his wife would be there that nite. I said what boss, forgetting. She meant the boss at the real estate office where she stenoged. I forgot she was still working there. So I gave her a big intro. and also gave her 2 more nos to sing than usual so she could impress her boss. Well I tho't no more of it till the next nite she was there early & said she wanted to talk to me

and I said o.k. and what she wanted to talk
about was dough and I tho't being innocent I
tho't she wanted to pay me back the sums I
advance to her but oh no. She said her boss
asked her how much she was getting and she
told him our arrangement about me coaching
her etc. So the heel went to the "owner" of the
joint because he (Herta's boss) handled the real
estate deal on the property and knew Lang, the
"owner." He found out Lang was giving me the
25 for Herta and so he wanted to know why I
didn't give her the 25 and put ideas in her head
that she should get the 25 less $2.50 for my
commission. $2.50!! my commission for teach-
ing her everything she ever knew. Anyway I
told her I said I had a little matter of a contract
and that stopped her but the next nite who
should come in but Martin the name of her boss
and Lang was also there, just before the joint
opened for the nite. I do not wish to bore you
with the details but dont let anybody tell you
they got rid of the muscle boys in Chi. because
we argued pro & con and finally I got mad and
said I have a contract with Herta and Martin
said let me see it & I showed it to him and right
before my two eyes he slowly tore it up. He
turn to Lang and said "I guess everything is
satisfactry now?" and Lang laughed. I saw I was
licked as those gorills do not care anything
about law and what was the use of me a stranger

trying to do anything. Then I said "Mr. Martin just what is yr. angle?" Meaning what, he replied. I said "Oh nothing but I sure do admire yr. nerve." Oh my nerve is o.k. he said. I have nothing to fear from a punk crooner like you. I said with a smile "Go ahead and insult me as much as you care to, Mr. Martin, but I was not referring to that. All I was referring to was yr. nerve the way you bro't your wife here to hear the little girl friend the office wife sing." With that he burned and came at me but I had a bottle in my hand under the table all the time he was talking & anyway Lang stopped him. Not because Lang likes me any more than Martin but a couple people came in while we were sitting there and the joint use to have a bad reputaton for 3 shootings they had there a couple years ago and Lang was told to keep his nose clean by the cops if he wanted to operate in that neighborhood as they did not want more complaints. "Oh well he is not worth brusing my knuckles on" said Martin and I laughed in his face and he went out.

Well Martin has something on Lang o.k. because I found out from the cashier that Herta is getting 50 now. The nerve of this Martin, he still brings his wife to the joint and Herta often goes & sits with Mrs. M. and she is old enough to be her mother, so I guess it is one of those things where a woman would rather have her husband chasing around after young girls just as long as he don't get a divorce. You cant tell me any different. I see it all too clear why I could not move in on Herta. These "innocent" ones are the ones alright. If I was a little more innocent maybe I would be right up there getting 2 grand a wk. etc.

Well Ted, give my love to everybody in 802 except about 5000 heels that all think that all they need is just a little 8 piece combinaton and they would have the best little band etc. etc. Drop me a line but be careful who you give my address to.

PAL JOEY

Joey on the Cake Line

FRIEND TED:

Well Xmas is coming and the geese are getting fat, please put a penny in the blind man's
hat as the old saying use to go but not that I am
asking you to put a penny in my hat or am not
a blind man either as far as that is concerned. I
never saw the day wherein no matter how
much moola I had I could not use some more
but I am saving you for a big touch in case I
want to start my own band in competition with
you (who knows I may be kidding on the level
and that would be quite irony if it ever happened?) I do not know why it is that I sound
like everything was sharp and I was right up
there because if you want the truth and the
whole truth and nothing but the truth your pal
Joey is on the cake line. That is my way of
putting it that I am on the bread line only I am
still a little better off. You get what I have reference to about cake & bread. It was a famous
historical topper when Josephine, the wife of
Napoleon was informed that the poor people

did not have any bread to eat and she said "Why dont they eat some cake if they havent any bread." Very good considering what they did was lop off her conk for saying it. Well I got my head lopped off too but not for making any crack. I went to the club one nite to give with the vocal chorus and add some class to the joint with my new midnite blue tails only there was no club there. That is the place was burn to the ground. 10,000 nite clubs in this country but I guessed they repealed the law of averages because they had to pick the one I was in to have a fire. I notice I never get that kind of odds when I go to the track. But who is complaning. I know one lug is complaning but will come to him later. So this nite I went there and all there was was ropes and fire hoses with ice hanging down and the joint stank worse than ever because you burn some rugs and pour some water on it and the water freezes to ice and you have some stink. Believe you me. Well there was nobody around but some firemen and a cop I know and the cop pointed to the joint and said to me "The hottest nite spot in Chicago" and I asked him what caused it and he said kiddingly "I guess some sparks from your singing." I have enough on him to crucify him but he lets me park anywhere so I did not report him. It seems I did not read the afternoon papers when I got up that afternoon and did not know there was

this fire. Well I finally got in touch with the
"owners" and they said act of God and fire etc.
wash up a contract automatically and I said to
them to wait a minute I did not have a contract.
I didnt either and I did not want them babies
to think they had me under contract because
another spot was making me offers but they did
not understand what I meant but tho't I was
going to try to hold them up for my week as it
was only a Tues. So they said "Joey you are the
1st one to come here and did not try to make
some trouble for us and with us you are a right
guy altho it is a pleasant surprise, even if we
would of had a contract we would not had to
pay you because of fire and act of God but let
us repeat you are a right guy and any time we
open up again we hire you before we even hire
a waiter." So I saw what they were thinking I
meant when I said I did not have a contract.
They were thinking I was giving them a break
so I said "Well what the hell, I said. I do not pretend I am some kind of a patsy but you fellows
always put it on the line for me every pay day
and gave me good billing so I did not want to
come here only to offer you my sympathy and
if I had some moola put away I would even lend
you some or any part of it to open up again."
One of them looked at the other and looked at
me and then at the other and said "Well, I have
seen everything" and then he stood up and

shook hands and said "As you know we are only the front men here as the backers do not wish to appear but as long as we are in this business one guy will always have a job and it is you Joey. How are you fixed?" So I said well you saw that new midnite blue tailcoat I just bo't I said that was not paid for only partly, just the down payment. I said you know how it is in this business a guy has to have a front and I would hate to lose that and they realized it and said they would give me my week right away and reached in his pocket and pealed of 5 20s, my week. I tho't I might as well give it to them but good so I said not if they couldnt spare it and they said that was alright. Then Solly the one fellow said he had been thinking it over and he had a little propositon for me and it was this. He said for me to keep going around to the good spots every nite and make contacts until they opened up again and then when they did I would still be a big attracton because people would not get the chance to forget me and get myself some publicity as much as possible and he would leave that to me. I started to say what would I use for moola and he said to me "I anticipate yr. queston. We in this business hate each others guts but we all have to co-operate with one another and all I have to do is call the boys that run the other joints and tell them I would apprisiate it providing they would not slap a couvert on you and I personally will give you 50 a wk to pay yr expenses, how does that look to you?" Well you know how it look to me. Getting paid for what I would do anyway so I shook on it and so that is what I am doing and do not have to worry about another job but am ruining the vocal chords smoking too much in joints and only singing once in a while when some m.c. says "I see we have another celebrity in our mist" and introduces me and I give. So that is why I am on the cake line not the bread line.

But will have to tell you a funny story like I hinted above regarding one fellow that is complaning. I did mention how I bo't this tailor-made tailcoat but only pd. the down payment. It is midnite blue and it fits me like a sword holder fits a sword. About a wk. before the joint burned down I got delivery on this tailcoat and had to con the tailor into letting me have it for only the down payment. All told it was to cost me $100. I put down a 25 down payment. But I said to him how can I pay you if you dont leave me wear it and I lose my job. So when they had the fire I went to him and said he could have it back as I could not pay for it and he yelled bloody murder and I walked out on him and said go ahead sue because you cannot garnishy my salary as I have no salary and any-way I am bankrupted. Im not but how does he know. So he had to take it back then I got a guy in the band with the same build I have and he went in to the same fellow and said he was thinking of having a tails made and the tailor did not know it was a friend of mine and he said "I have just the thing for you. A customer did not call for this" proving he was a crook. My pal said well he wanted one more conservative not blue but the tailor said "I will tell you what I will do I will let you have it for $65 the latest thing." My friend said he was not thinking of paying that kind of money and anyway he could get a ready made for 40. So the tailor came down to 45 and my pal said okay. He took it. So I gave my pal a fin for his acting ability and so all told I got my tailcoat for a total of 75. They always overcharge you anyway those tailors because they figure on losing dough when they give credit and bad debts etc. So I just paid him what the damn thing was worth altho on me it is very becoming as they say in that gag.

I guess you got my Xmas card. A funny thing. I ordered two kinds this Xmas, the kind I sent you and also the conservative ones with very formal Greetings of the Season and a stage coach & four and my name engraved on it. They were for the Onawentsia Club crowd friends but "accidentally" I got one of the ones I sent you in the envelope with the stage coach ones and now I understand the whole town is talking about the amusing cards. Everybody wanted to know who posed for it. Nobody did as the fellow that drew it copied it out of *Esquire* but I just look wise when anybody says they think it was so and so or this one or that. It certainly got me plenty publicity.

Well Merry Christmas, as the saying goes. Guess I will have to go to bed for 24 hrs so I dont have to stop hating my fellow men. But that does not go for you, Ted. The best.

PAL JOEY.

The Erloff

FRIEND TED:

In my prevous communicaton I informed you how I guess it was some critic of singing set fire to the joint I was singing in and I was out of a job. I am only kidding about the place being set fire by a music critic because what I hear the singing in Chicago does not have any high standards to achieve (sneeze when you say that Pal). They tell me it is been going on for years but I only just heard about the singers here, how what you do is get some guy that his idea of music is when he heard them sticking the little pigs in their throat down at the stock yards, which is plenty loud and plenty high (especially high at the stock yards if you get what I referring to and hold yr. nose at that gag). That is their idea of music and the 1st thing you know they are knocking themselves out indevouring to sign some baby that sings loud and high and sign her up to sing opera. At but all the moola a week anybody can spend not excepting I. Had I but known of this at an earlier age I would of made the nessary preparatons and arrangements and wd. be a soprano now at plenty moola a wk. instead of being somewhere between Frankie Parker outdoors on a rainy nite and the Groaner giving an imitaton of a cry of joy or scared of a mouse.

I told you I had this deal with my ex-boss, 50 a wk to go around the other joints and make an appearance so the public wd not forget me until my boss opened up again. Well I had this little mouse, a very nice little spivot that belong to the college crowd at the Northwestern U. I think you played a job there two yrs ago at a "prom" so you know about it. They have some nice mice out there and she was one. I had her out this nite and over came a chap I say hello to occasonally, and he is a member of the Saddle & Cycle Club. Alright I am kidding you and this is 1939 or 1940 (I have not got it straight yet) and they do not have any club name the Saddle & Cycle only they do!!! 1940! Anyway this is a rich playboy type of a chap and kind of an Ed. Arnold type. He does all the talking so I do not have to tell him any lies and when he saw me and this mouse he said to join him as they are going slumming. Slumming was what he said and slumming was what he meant. From one of the top rooms in Chi we go bang to a joint that is a joint. The mouse with me is strictly no cigar and the daughter of a small town banker in

Indiana and have a summer home up in Mich, and I am thinking of next summer when I take her out. So she is not the one I would of pick to go with me to a joint like the one we went. But she said she wanted to go and when I said yes her guess was as good as mine where we were heading. Strictly a bruhaha. But Sat. nite! This guy that took us is well known or else I would of turned around the minute we got there. In we go. Wide open like a movie of a mining camp town. An ugly old hag of an Irish lady is yelling for help altho using the words of I Want the Waiter with the Water and accompanied by maybe her uncle or maybe her son, a man that should of been in bed hrs ago. I am not kidding. He thumped out the bass and drank his beer at the same time and it was not on purpose. I mean it was not a gay 90 gag. They were leveling. So pretty soon our party got seated at our table and this little old guy came over and I tho't here is an old guy and in a minute he is going to take out a piece of rope and ask the gentlemen to tie him up and inside of 2 minutes he will be free. That was what he looked like. But when he came over to our table Preston stood up and shook hands with him and introduced everybody to him and told him to sit down which he did. Well his name was Paddy Dunlin and all he is is the owner of the joint. Not only of this particular joint but about 50 other ones. I do not wish to get ahead of my story but in plain words the old corpse has girls anyway from two bits to whatever you want to pay for. And the face of a saint as they say. Anyway he sat down next to me and had a beer on Preston and when the other members of our party got up to dance, he looked me over and then he whispered to me "What about the erloff." I said what a couple of times. I finally caught on that he was asking me what about the little mouse. Oh, nothing, I said. "Slumming" he said. Then he said "What do you think of the erloff" and this time I did not say what but watched him. He made a gesture with his head and his expression and that meant he was ask-ing me what did I think of the joint. I stalled to think of something and he had to go away to answer the phone and Preston came back to the table and gave me some facts on the old guy. He said I was not in Chi long enough to know about him. He said the old guy was over 70 and was running joints from the time he was 21 yrs of age. There was a story around that when they had that bank holiday one of the railroad cos had to come to the old guy for cash. He had over 2 million in cash. Hotels, railroads, all the respectable big cos had to come to him for cash. He said (Preston) how for yrs every morning the sisters came around and collected choice meats like steaks & chops etc. that was left over from the nite before, and took it away and gave it to the poor. Also potatoes and salad and red beets etc. Also butter and bread. The works. Every single morning. He was always good for a roof on a church just as long as it was Catholic. He buried thousands of people that would of been buried in the potter's field if he did not get up the dough. Charity after charity. But then they gave an order that nobody was to take any more from the old guy. It made him sad and he almost began hitting the sauce, but his elderly wife would not allow him in the house with boose on his breath so he just did not drink.

I listened attentively because Preston was paying for the party but if you want the truth I was bore to death with Preston and with his old charachter. That was what Preston called him a fascinating old charachter. To me he was a dirty old man with a lot of moola. I was even thinking rapid calculation how much it would cost to take my little mouse out of her sororty house by taxi instead of waiting till Preston decide to take us home and just then the old man returned from his phone call. He must of got a big order from some Amer. Leg. conventon because he was smiling when he sat down with us.

The old dame got up again and began horsewhipping The Lamp is Low. Dunlin said to me "How do you like the erloff" and I said fine.

Great I said. "Right" he said. "She is been with me fifteen yrs." And I thought to myself yes and you must of looked her over a long time before hiring her too. Her and the band been with me 15 yrs he said. I said that was wonderful these days to have such loyalty going on but to myself I tho't yes you all stick together to keep warm like old cows out on the range during a blizzard. I had a look at the band. He had them hid behind some palms but there was one old guy playing cornet that looked as if he was worried for fear that the Confederates wd catch him for being a deserter. "The erloff, they like the erloff" said Dunlin. Everything was erloff with this decrept old bore and I was thinking to myself 2 million cash, old man or no old man, he is driving me nuts so I am going to break a 5 dollar bill over some hack driver's head and take my little mouse home in a taxi but I am glad I didn't because just then the old man says to me "Of course in the Loop you got a different erloff Joey." I said what? "The erloff, he said. They like noise here and that's the way I like it. You would just as well come wearing a shell if you ever took a job in a spot like this, that is how big an egg you would lay. But the class people that go to the rooms you been working in like hardly any noise at all." Well he called me Joey and I was figuring all the while he tho't I was a Cycle Club boy but no. He made me the minute he saw me, as the detectives say. He said he understood I was a sock the last 2 rooms I worked and right out in front of the little mouse he said 100 a wk was not enough for a handsome young chap that could put over a ballad and have the women with their tongue hanging out. "Don't worry, he said when you open up again you will be getting one five 0. You also have a nice personality for that kind of a room." I said I certainly would apprisiate him giving me a plug with the owners and he looked at me and said "Are you kidding? *I* own that joint." Then he got up and walked away and I was too surprise to think for a minute and tho't I plumbered it but we have opened up again in another room and I am getting one five o. The erloff Pal.

Always your
PAL JOEY

Even the Greeks

FRIEND TED:

I don't think I will be able to take it out here much more. In the 1st place it is because you never saw cold weather until you spent a winter in Chi. I do not mean weather like you have to chop the alcohol before putting it in the radator of the car. I mean weather that is so cold that the other day this pan handler came up to me and braced me and said I look as if I had a warm heart and I gave him a two-bit piece because if it wasnt for him would not of known I was alive or frozen to death. That was how it has been here in Chi. Maybe that explains some of the pecular actons of many of the inhabitants. Illinois is a state of suspended animaton and the people live in hibernaton from Oct. to whenever it ever gets warmer. I do not know and hope I am not here long enough to find out. I am merely telling you this in case you ever decide to take a job to spend the winter in Chi and I am not there to stop you at the point of a gun.

Well if you think I am trying to infer that I have been running up against some of the pecularities of the local natives you will only be 100% correct. The club opened up again after the fire as you no doubt read here or there like in the *Variety* or the *Down Beat*. We got off to good business but that was to be expect it. It wd of surprised me had it been otherwise so only menton it in passing. What I want to tell you is about the pecular local people and this one case. Two wacks if I ever saw one and they are Nick the prop. of the Olympia rest. and Pete that works for him in the kitchen. The Olympia is on my way home when I am on my way home if you know what I mean.

I just as soon never go home but a man has to have his rest so when I go home ever since I have been living where I now am I use to stop in at the Olymp. for a coffee and raison cake before going to bed. I got to be a regular customer there and Nick would expect me to come in around 3,4 in the morning so as to relive the monotony with a wise crack or two and I guess Nick was very grateful to me because one nite I heard somebody out in the kitchen yell "right" and a minute or two later out through the hole in the wall bet. kitchen and rest. a plate slid and on the plate was some food. Nick was just about going to throw it in the garbage and then he noticed me and he said "could you use a ham omlet?" I said sure. So he gave me the ham omlet, or what ever it was. I asked him what was wrong with it but he said nothing was wrong and go ahead and eat it if I preferred to. So I ate it and it was as good a ham omlet as I ever ate.

A nite or so after I went in Nick's again and was having a cup of coffee and once more I heard somebody out in the kitchen yell "right" and a couple minutes later out came a jelly omlet and once more Nick looked at me and said could I eat a jelly omlet and I said I could force one and he assured me that there was nothing phony about it but go ahead and eat it and it was as good a jelly omlet as any jelly omlet I ever ate.

Then I went in the next nite and ordered a coffee and waited but Nick didn't offer me anything. Then the nite after that I went in and sure enough somebody out in the kitchen yelled "right" and in a minute or so out came a beautiful club sandwich. Nick asked me again could I use a club sandwich and I said I tho't may be I could and it was a tasty club sandwich which I enjoyed to the hilt. So that was the way it went. Some nites hungry and not wishing to throw away a dollar I wd go to Nick's hoping to get an omlet or tasty sandwich but no cigar. I wd not get a thing. Other nites I wd go in and get like a small steak one nite. But I began to notice one thing. The only times I got a free meal it was when the fellow out in the kitchen suddenly yelled out "right." Nobody wd order anything but he wd yell it and then in a minute or two something very tasty wd come through the opening. So naturally I wd wait around hoping this fellow in the kitchen wd yell "right" because if he did that meant I wd get a free meal. So all the time naturally I was helping Nick relive the monotony by chatting about this and that and one night the usual thing. The fellow yelled, out came liver & bacon and Nick just looked at me and at the liver & bacon and I said sure. Then my curosity got the better of me and I asked him. I said "Nick what's with the free food? Explain." So he said eat my liver and bacon and he wd explain the entire mystery. So I ate it and then he said to look out in the kitchen and I wd see a husky well built man about 50 yrs of age sweeping up or polishing pots and pans. That is Peter, said Nick. "Pete use to be the best short order cook I ever ran across in all my experience in this business. But one day Pete's wife ran away with a wrestler and took their three little ones with them and Pete began hitting the sauce and got into a fight and somebody hit him over the conk with a bung starter and he was never the same after that. But Nick knew Pete as boys in the old country and Nick made up his mind that Pete wd always have a job as long as he owned a rest. So Nick had to hire another cook and gave Pete the job sweeping up. But every once in a while while sweeping up Pete wd think he heard Nick order something like a ham omlet or small steak or one of the other dishes that Pete was good at and he wd put down his broom and go and cook the omlet or whatever he tho't he heard. Oh and I forgot to say in there that when he wd think he wd hear Nick ordering he wd yell out 'right' and then start cooking it. I said to Nick that must run into money. Yes, it does, said Nick but that is okay and anyway you are here to eat the stuff so I do not have to throw it away."

Well that is all about Nick and Pete and I do not know which one is wackiest either Nick for keeping Pete or Pete himself. You can make up your mind as I have my own idea. But that is the way they are in this town. Even the Greeks.

Your

PAL JOEY

Joey and the Calcutta Club

PAL TED:

Well, Chum, the poor man's Bing Crosby is still making with the throat here in Chi. but if the present good fortune keeps up I ought to be getting the New York break pretty soon. The trouble is up to now the good fortune has been keeping so far up it is up in the stratuspere out of sight. But never out of mind, kiddy. Never out of mind. N.Y. is where I belong N.Y. or Hollywood or will settle for both. However have been off the bread line and working steady but you do not see me on the caviare line yet and was always a one to have the ambiton to starve to death within reach of caviare if you get what I mean. If I have to starve to death it would be this way, namely, have about 5 lbs of caviare and filet mignon & champagne etc. but me too God damn lazy to reach for it. Maybe to make it perfect I would be firsting my attentons on like Hedy La Marr instead of just plain lazy and would be so busy would forget to eat. That is the manner in which I would prefer to starve to death.

Well, speaking of the charming opposite sex I
have a little spot of annecdotes (I dote on
annecdotes) to tell you which may amuse the
chappies around Lebuses and give them all my
best excepting those that I would not say I
would not spit on them as I can hardly wait to
spit on them. Well this is the story and not only
a story but also a good thing to keep in mind in
case you get in the same situaton some time
yourself.

Shortly after I got started working here, a little mouse came in one nite with a party of six
and naturally began asking for request nos. and
in that way I got aquainted and also thru knowing one of the guys on the party. It was not a
spending party, strictly cufferoo. The guy is a
fellow named Quinn on one of the local papers
here in Chi. and covers nite clubs, etc. and signs
his initials L. Q. to reviews he gives the spots
here & there but mostly in the Loop etc. So
Quinn asked me to join them and I did and this
mouse with them named Jean Benedict looks
like 10000 other dames on the line of some
Bway show except when she opens her trap she
has an accent that is so British even Sir Nevile
Chamberlin would not be able to understand
her. I knew she was strictly U.S.A. by appearance but the accent is so good I think what is
the angle. What gives, I asked her, altho not in
so many words. I inquired how she happen to

have the accent and she said a lot of people inquire of her the same thing and it is easily explained. She is half American and her father is British. Well she sounded so refined I wanted to say a few one syllable words to her to note the effect to see if she would know what I meant. Well I did not, not that nite. About three nites later. The 1st nite all she did was to say why didn't I call her up at her flat and drop in for a gin and "it." I said the "it" was o.k. with me if we were both talking about the same thing and she put on the act as if not getting "it" and then said priceless. Oh, how wrong she was when she said priceless but am getting ahead of my story.

Well on acc't of a certain other obligaton which I mentoned in my prevous letter I could not give my full attention to Miss Benedict but will just say in passing if I would of given her any more attenton at the rate I was going I would now not be cutting paper dolls. Oh no. I would not be able to lift a paper doll. However let me suffice it to say that I moved in & during the course of our more dull conversatons I accertain that Miss Benedict is living with this other mouse whom I do not meet. They are sharing this flat. Also she tells me her dear mother and dear papa are in dear old London. I never asked her that. All I asked her was did she live alone, etc. and now I recall it she certaintly did jump at the chance to explain about the old man and the mother. I should of known that the English have more reserve about personal affairs but I guess I had good reason to forget all about reserve in connecton with Miss B. Anyway she gave me the routine about father & mother being in London that day and two days later when "love dropped in for tea" meaning me, she kept standing by the window and looking out and when I would say anything to her she would act like as if she did not hear me and then I finally said pardon me but remember me I am yr. pal Joey, the fellow that just came in about 15 mins. ago and didnt we meet at the club etc. She said "I apologize" but she was upset and maybe it would be better if I did not stay but went out to a picture that day as she was not herself. I must say the girl is an actress because I honestly tho't I squeezed it out of her that her check from her old man was late and she said no doubt because of the way things have been in dear old London. She said she always got her check of $300 by the 7th of the month, sometimes earlier depending on how soon the boats arrived from London. But here it was the 10 or 11 of the month and no check and no letter either. The check always came with a letter and she worried about if they sent her father off on some misson for the gov't and it was so important he was not allowed to leave

her know he was even going away. He was some
important fellow in the office that runs India
and maybe they sent him there. It was not only
the money but what if it was an important dan-
gerous misson? What about her mother, I
inquired? Well, she said that was where she
swore me to secrecy and told me that her
mother was an American but also had a lot to
do with India, also some kind of an agent but
American in name only so as to keep her pass-
port. Well of course all this went on for a half
an hr. and eventually I was a sucker for the
touch. I admit it. I let her have $75.

Well I gave her my oath I would not tell
about her people being sort of spies against
India but even so would not of told anybody
about it as I did not want it to get around that
I went for a $75 touch as you get the reputaton
of being a soft touch like that and pretty soon
girls from all over the country are waiting at yr.
dressing room and also I had this "other obligaton" if *she* heard I was putting out 75 here and
there she would take back her car and maybe
even get me the bounceroo from this spot. So I
kept quite but one nite soon after I happen to
see Quinn and went over to thank him for a
nice menton and he started out by asking me
how was Miss Benedict. I played dumb and he
said, "Oh, I tho't you were in. I took for granted
you were in and how did you happen to miss

that as I was given to understand that you are a young man that moved right in." Well imagine. I burned and said "Listen, wise guy not only am I in but the nite you bro't her here she slipped me her phone no. with you sitting at the table." I could of cut my throat when I realized what I said, insulting the guy after he gave me he good notice but instead he did not get sore. On the contrary he replied, "Ah, then perhaps you will join our little club. What did she take you for?" I said for nothing. And he said "Oh, you can level with me, do you mean to say she did not put the touch on you for a little, like a yard?" So I admitted it and then he told me. It seems that I was a member of quite a club, and a paid up member too. Miss B. took Quinn for 50 and another guy for 50 and another for 75 and one guy for around 300, a middle aged fellow that sold religious articles to churches and did not want any trouble. So Quinn said we ought to form a club called the Calcutta Club after the town over in India. Well I saw the humor of it but I would of liked to give Miss B. a kick in the stomach if she came along at the time.

Well I put it down to experence and tho't no more of it till about two wks. later Quinn came in and told me he had a propositon, not his but Miss B.'s. It seems what she did was take our India money and move out and get a more expensive flat by herself without the girl friend and after she moved in she was there about two weeks and met some guy from Milwaukee that tho't she was right and so much so that this guy was already talking wedding bells even before he moved in. She had him thinking it made her sick to see a woman smoke and she never went out to nite spots but always had a good book around. How she picked him up I dont know but he was going for everything. He had no sus-picons aroused because at the time she was absolutely staying away from the spots. Well she only had two wks. to go she told Quinn before the rent was due and that meant only two wks. to work on the prospect from Milwaukee, so the propositon she put to Quinn was if we would stake her to the next month's rent and she felt sure that was all she would need. He asked me what I tho't of it and he said frankly he had not $50 to throw away but he would rather throw the 50 away on a chance of getting the 100 back and he advised me to do same. He won me over but I told him on one conditon, namely, how did we know that was this sucker from Milwaukee and so it was agreed that if she could produce him and convince us then we would put up the ready. So that was how it was and a nite or two later she came in the club and him with her and I took one quick gander at him and was convinced but to make sure I stopped at the table suddenly like I just recognized him and said, "I beg yr. pardon but havent we met. I am sure I met you in Milwaukee last yr." and the way he got red and said no I knew he was from Milwaukee and I also knew something Miss B. did not know as smart as she was, namely, he was dumb but not that dumb that he would marry her, but was willing to put up the rent etc. Well that was o.k. She pretend to go to the little girls rm. and I had a talk with her and told her I was in favor of the propositon and would tell the other members of the club I was and she would have the front money. But I also told her that Mr. Milwaukee was not going to marry her if I knew human nature and she said to me, "Joey, darling, I could almost like you for being so intelligent, if for nothing else." She said "I told Quinn that Chubby (the nickname for the Milwaukee guy) did not move in but he did move in but Quinn is a dope and I had to tell him a good story. What I want the front money for is so Chubby will get expensive ideas and not get the idea that he is only going for coffee and cakes dough." Then she gave me a little kiss on the cheek and said "that will have to be all for the present but we shall see what we shall see." So the boys got their dough back last wk. including me but I got mine in three 50 dollar bills inclosed in a gold clip with a watch on it. You have to admire a girl like that from Buffalo, N.Y. where she is from. That is how English she is. She has relatons in Canada. Anyway she is a very smart little operator and I predict great things for her. She got me putting on a little wt. as Chubby likes caviare and she always keeps some in the frigidair for him but all we singers put on wt. like Caruso, McCormick, Crosby, etc.

Yrs.
PAL JOEY

Joey and Mavis

FRIEND TED:

I do not wish this to constitute a regular letter as am only setting down my tho'ts at random more or less as they come to me sitting here casually after dinner while Mavis is at the movies with the kids. Perhaps a few words about Mavis would not be a miss as I have had so many things happen to me since writing you before that I did not get the opportunity to inform you regarding Mavis who has bro't such changes into my life that I can not believe it myself when I stop to think of it.

It happened one nite (from the picture of the same name) and I just finished a set and was outside on the sidewalk in front of the joint filling up my lungs with Gods air & some of my own cigarette smoke instead of 50 other people's and was talking to the doorman Sailor Bob a punchy stumble-bum that after 20 yrs learned how to open the door of that new inventon the auto but did not catch on how to close it. I use to go out and stand there & leave him pay me a few compliments on my voice as he tho't himself a great hand as a singer. He could not of been a worse fighter than a singer otherwise he would of been worm meat 20 yrs ago or more and none of this would of happened. He apprisiated my singing I will say that for him altho always asking why didnt I sing like Oh you beautiful doll which you are too young to remember and so am I but the story I hear is that when the Titanic went down (a ship) people sang it or hummed a couple bars and then said the hell with this and jumped the hell off the boat so they would not have to finish singing it. I do not know that for sure but only base that on hearsay based on a weak moment when I allowed the Sailor to sing it for me one nite. I tho't why does this happen to me, everything happens to me. I tho't I was the poor man's good Samaratan to listen to that but was glad later as one nite I was on my way out and some guy that had suspicons of me & his wife was waiting for me and I was doing some very fast talking when out of the corner of my eye I saw the Sailor and yelled to him and I must say that what the Sailor can not do with his fist he does not have to do as he does it with the boot. I have seen some dirty fighting in my travels with the socialites and polo players I grew up with but nothing to compare with the Sailor who is a pleasure to watch work if you care for that sort of thing and I do especially when he is working on somebody that a minute ago was going to stick their fist down my throat. Anyway the guy had the wrong party as it was not me but the drummer in the band. I had her sister and it was not even the right nite he was referring to.

Well as I started in to say this one nite I went out and the Sailor was on duty and I was more less fronting for him that is on smoking. He was not allow to smoke on duty but it was o.k. for me to so I would say "I will light one for you Sailor" and if the mgr. came out the Sailor would hand it to me and would not get caught smoking on duty. Then this 1937 La Salle sedan came up and four got out, two couples. The fellow driving asked if it would be o.k. to park here and the Sailor working for a tip stalled and said not as a rule but in this case etc. so the fellow driving gave him a buck and they went inside. I do not know how I happen to miss Mavis but I did not see her until I had to go in again and polish off some more dittys and they had a table ringside, and I went over and asked them if they had any request nos. and Mavis asked for two requests but did not have both of them only the Beguin no. The other was an oldy like My Buddy which they were singing during the civil war. I know it but forgot the lyrics. She looked around 32 or 33, inclined to take on a little weight but I also like them zoftick as some goose in the band says. They asked me to sit down with them and join them in a drink but I could not have a drink on the job but we got into conversaton and in the course of the conversaton she happen to menton that when she saw me outside talking to the doorman she tho't perhaps I was there waiting for a date instead of working in the joint and she meant it as a compliment as she said this spot was new to her and she did not like to go to strange spots but thinking I was the type customer the joint got she figured it was o.k. I said I considered her a very wise person and I was not kidding because all the time I kept looking at her I kept adding up how much she had on her was worth. At least a two-caret diamond ring on the engagement finger and also a diamond bracelet and a gold cigarette case with inside it (not outside) her three initials in diamonds M. W. K. (for Mavis Williams Ketchell but did not find that out till later). The people with her were in their 40s. Well I always make it a point to leave a table while they still want me to stay (always leave them laughing) so I moved away and merely said I hope they would come again etc. I could not figure out any way how to get her phone no. without asking for one on the chin. I had some preminiton that I could move in if I played it right but was also not sure. I could not figure if maybe one of the two guys bo't those diamonds or if she had her own dough or if she was a wealthy young divorcee or young widow or what the hell? She was so cagey that all I knew about her was all she wanted to let me know. Even so I had the preminiton that once I got alone with her I would let her do the talking and maybe she would talk herself into it.

Well I went out again for a smoke and of course asked the Sailor who own the La Salle but he never saw it before and I could not get any clue but just then fate fell into my hands. At first I tho't my luck ran out because here they were all coming out, Mavis & the other three. The one fellow backed up the sedan and the others got in and then when they were all in the other dame decided she wanted to sit in back with "Harry" and Mavis got out and the other dame got in the back and sat with Harry and Mavis started to get in front with the other guy and just when she was sitting down the Sailor must of decided that the important thing was on the seat because just then he slammed the door and got her right foot. She let out one "Jesus H. Christ" and then I saw her face and she was biting her lower lip in pain. Trying to keep from crying I guess but very couragous. Then when she had a look at her foot she passed out and I damn near did too. The Sailor put everything in that slam and it would take your appetite away to describe her foot. I saw it all happen.

Well plenty of excitement. The mgr. came out and the Sailor was non compass mentis and did not know what to do and the other dame was screaming like she was the one that had the door slammed on her own foot instead of Mavis. They finally got a dr. and they took Mavis to a hospital. One of the guys in the car took my name etc. and all I could think of was that fixed it fine as far as Mavis coming back to the joint for a while or maybe ever. The way her foot looked it would be lucky if she did not lose the foot. But it was not as bad as I tho't and a day or two later a guy came around to my place and asked me a lot of questons about how it happened. He was from the ins. co. he said and I tho't he meant the ins. co. that Mavis was insured by but no, he was from the one that covered the joint for accidents like that. I told him a story that should of got Mavis $1,000,000. The next wk. I got the bounceroo from the joint. It seems that they settled with Mavis for around $1100 but if I would of had a different story ready maybe they could of got away without settling for anything. I still dont know all the angles and do not give a damn. I told the mgr. if I knew what kind of a story he wanted me to tell maybe I would of told a different one but he said it was just too bad but they did settle. I was out and also the Sailor.

But I guess the Sailor can always get himself a spot in some gym but there I was with only about $85 in my poke and no job. So I was desperate and almost wired you to put the touch on you but at the last moment got this idea and decided to call on Mavis at the hosp. I did so and much to my pleasant surprise was told to go right up to room whatever it was. She was surrounded with flowers and was glad to see me instead of giving me the brush which was what I was afraid of. She had her foot in a plaster cast and first she made me feel at home and then said for me to take a pencil and write my name on the cast as she understood I saw the whole thing and must of told the truth about how it happened otherwise they would not of settled so quickly. "Yes," I said. "I was too truthful for my own good, Mrs. Ketchell, as they discharged me because I was ready to go to court and tell the truth that the doorman was to blame for the unfortunate accident." She tho't a minute and said she wished she knew that at the time before settling, however she asked me to sign my autograph on the cast and I did.

Well we chatted and she asked me to come and see her again and I said I would be happy to as I would have plenty of time and she said that was perfect because most of her friends

worked in the day time and she did not have
many woman friends in Chicago that could
come and call on her and it was such a bore in
the hospital alone. So I started going there every
day and soon she told me the story of her life
and how she was so happy with her two children and husband but one day he came home
and shot himself and the ins. co. had to pay double because that was in the clause and she could
not bear to live in the small town where her
home was because it was too full of memories
so she came to Chi. Her husband was 20 yrs
older than she and she was hardly more than a
girl when she got married but even so was
happy with him as he did every thing in the
world for her. Well I can tell you one thing in
the world he did not do for her because I am
no 20 years older than she is and no old guy 50-
some years old did everything in the world for
her. They could attach a wire to her and I bet
she could light up a city of 50,000 populaton
the way they did with some ship out on the
Coast. After she got out of the hospital she got
me to take a room near where she has an apartment for herself & the two kids. She knows a
guy that is going to back a new joint in the
Loop dist. and when the thing is ready I am
practically set to open there and meanwhile we
go out about every nite. I caught her in a few
lies but this is on the level and I think she has

something on the guy that is backing the new spot as one nite we were on our way in a place and he was standing there waiting and she said to him, "How nice to see you, Tom" and introduced me and said I was just the singer for the new spot and he began to stall and she said not to bore her but just make an appointment with me and he said "Oh, is it that way?" and she replied "Why, Tom darling, just what do you mean?" and laughed and he said o.k. and I see him next Tues. I sure would hate to let her get anything on me.

Well she ought to be back soon and I want to put this in the envelope and seal it up and when she sees I was writing to a guy and not some dame it should make her a happy girl. Age 37 if I can believe her drivers license.

I wonder what the poor people are doing?

Regards
PAL JOEY

A New Career

FRIEND TED:

By the business we are doing these nites one wd never be let to suspect that there is a world conflagraton going on but nevertheless such is the case. The rope is up every nite of the wk except Monday and then such is the kind of lug I am working for that he wants to put the rope up and hang himself from it because one nite of the wk maybe four tables do not get occupied by people buying wine. This is the same guy that I recall distintly six months ago if 4 tables did happen to be occupied he wd spent $40 phoning his girl on the road with some band that business was terrific. Now when he gets a bad nite he thinks it is brutal.

I guess you are wondering why I am giving you these physical details. Well I do not blame you because why should you give a good God damn about some crib in Chicago even if I do happen to be working there. Of course I always give a damn if it is you and I understand you are going to be booked into the N.Y. Paramount in a couple wks and whoever's record is tops I hope you break it and am sure you will. But of course why you should care if we do 8000 or 800 except that I have a little propositon that may arouse yr interest and it is this.

I will tell you all about it and how I happen to have my interest aroused. It is owing to those Monday nites. My boss is known by the name Harry Bonbon which is a mob nickname he got from the mobsters not because of him liking chocolate bon-bon candy but his name was Burnbaum and they had a mobster with an impedima in his speech and the closest he could come to the name was Bonbon. That is one version. However that is as good as any and I just wanted to tell you his name Harry Bonbon. So these Monday nites he just sits there chewing on the end of his cigar (personally I wish he would chew on the lit end but no such luck) and he counts the empties and then I see him looking around and he will call a headwaiter and point to some lights and say "Save that" and the headwaiter will have to go out and turn off the light. He keeps doing that until by the time it gets to be 12 or half past the place is like a black out over in France. It is a very handy thing for the out of town spenders that have some local mouse out for the first time and want to find out if she has a wooden leg. It also is a very fine thing in favor of the light finger

gentery and I told Harry one Monday I said in
case he was interested over there was a bump
man I use to see out at the track some times and
I said maybe he is now working alone but it will
be a fine thing for the joint in case he happens
to bump into one of the socialites and the
socialites lose a handsome wallet stuffed with a
liberal supply of folding. "Jesus!" said Harry. I
never tho't of that and ordered the lights turned
on. Of course he has only been in this business
since around 1885, and should know by this
time that any time the socialites go out they
leave there folding money at home or most of
it. My experence with socialites is they go to a
spot with the expectaton of throwing away up
to $3 if it is a party of 2 or 4.

Well that is just an illustration of what I mean
about Monday nite and how Harry worries. If
it is not the lights it is go easy on the ice or use
napkins instead of fresh table clothes. Or go
easy on the air conditioning or no fresh packs
of matches but use old packs with one match in
them or else he is got the cashier going nuts
because he wants a report every 15 min. So of
course I also noticed another thing more
important than the above. I happen to notice
him one nite looking at me. He did not say anything. He merely looked. But the way he looked
was the way the head man looks on one of those
artic expeditons after nobody had anything to

eat for a wk. They are going around bare-footed
because they have used up their mocassins for
scoff. Maybe one of the chaps has knawed off a
nice juicey thumb. But the head man is looking
at me. I am the fat one (I did not put on any wt
but this is just an illustraton). I am say the radio
operator and got fat sitting around on the way
North and the head man thinks and thinks and
pretty soon he has no doubts about if he is
going to eat me. All he is wondering is will I
take much salt. Sunday nite they can have me
for cold cuts. That is the way Harry is looking
at me. Does he give a damn if I am the only one
that can operate the radio and notify civiliza-
ton? No. He is thinking I wd make a nice roast.
The same with Harry. Is he thinking about the
mice that come in because I work here? No. All
he is thinking is how if I was not on the payroll
it wd be the same as getting his electricity free.

Well I am a great student of human nature
and always prided myself on reading characters,
so I know Harry wd break my contract in a
minute. If I was not willing to break my contract then he wd get a couple of hoods and I wd
be in a taxi accident and maybe break my knee
cap. I will break a contract any day in preference
to my knee cap. So I sound out a couple other
spots but they say I want too much money. I
got desparate. I even went to one lug and said
I wd sing and run the floor show and also take

pictures. I did not have any kodak but anybody can take pictures but even so they said no and I wd not come down in price more than $25 a wk.

Well, what is an angle, I asked myself. Then because I always use to make my Easter duty and did a lot of people favors I got my reward. They had this busboy named Pablo that use to fix me up a sandwich once in a while and I befriended him by overhearing a tip on a horse at Arlington and it paid I think around $18.40 and Pablo was on it for a fin. So he always recalled that and one nite after Harry gave me the explorer look I was having a sandwich and I guess I was unable to disguise my feelings because Pablo ask me what was the matter and I just said nothing at all really. Just blue. And he tho't it was some mouse but I said any time a mouse made me feel that way he should let me know. I did not wish to worry Pablo and did not inform him why I was worried as I knew Pablo would worry too because even if he did not know it his job was also in danger and I wanted the poor chap to have his happiness. Well he took away the dishes etc. and you know how those people are and how nothing gets them down for long. They bounce right back because they are primitive and not very close to civilizaton like jigs. So a minute after he was so sympatico Pablo was humming away a tune.

Well I was smoking and thinking and suddenly this tune gradually began creeping into my thot's. It grew on me. Finally I asked him I said what was the name of it and he smiled and said it did not have any name. I said was it perhaps some Mexican folks' song and he said oh, yes, it was six or seven Mexican folks' songs all in one. He said it was one of his own, which he made up out of a lot of songs from his native land, Mexico. "Sing it again," I said. He was very pleased and sang it all through for me. Well I jumped up and as soon as the band finish the set I went over to the piano and one fingered it and wrote it out on the back of a menu card. But that was not necessary because on the way home I remembered it and the next afternoon when I woke up I remembered it.

Well you know how I am. Like Berlin. I can fake a tune in one key so the next couple days I was down at the joint in the afternoon playing it on the piano till I had it all mastered and not any too soon I might ad. Because the last afternoon I turned around and saw the guitar player in the band standing there. "How long of you been here," I said. He said he just got there and I did not know whether to believe him or not as he wd steal my tune as quick as look at me but I did not want to let on it was important so I just said play a few and he was like any ham musician and started in and played Muddy

Waters. I wanted to test him to see if he wd play my tune but he didn't.

Well now I have something in case Harry the explorer decides to cut me up but the hell of it is I cant trust any of these bastards and that is where you come in. I know there is no larceny in you Ted boy so what I am going to do is go to a music store and get one of those recording machines and play the tune and cut a wax of it. I will cut a couple and send one to you so that if you lose it or anything I will still have one and anyway that will show that it was my idea. Then when I send it to you you play it over and see if you think it has possibilities and if so maybe you can get Johnny Mercer or somebody to write some lyrics for it. I will guarantee to let you play it first over the air and who knows but perhaps that is not a new career for me, that of song writer. I have a lot of ideas along this line and only need a little encouragement. My tune can be played as either a rumba or conga, fox trot or waltz. If I could get a good Ascap rating this year I would quit this business in a minute and stop worrying about Harry the explorer. So look in the mail any day now for a record. Be sure and tell your secretary that anything from me is to go to you without opening it.

As always,
PAL JOEY

A Bit of a Shock

FRIEND NED:

Well Ted it may come like a bolt out of the blue sky me calling you Ned after all these years of you and I being mutual pals but why I called you Ned is because I wanted to prepare you for a surprise just like I got one about 2 wks ago. I had this little surprise around 2 weeks ago that I guess I certainly had it coming to me. In the ordinary course events a surprise comes from where you the least expect it and which is precisely what happened in my case. But dont worry as I do not intent to continue calling you Ned as you are Ted to me and the same old Ted and the same old pal Joey.

I menton above how where you least expect it etc. That goes double in spades and cards whatever that means. By double I mean in the 1st place *where*. The second place should be *how* and the third pl. *who*. Well where was a new crib where they had me rehearsing for a new show. I dreamed up a little comedy patter and a few stories like Joe E. Lewis and his little story about his cousin and the hot ferryboat but I guess I shouldnt of attempted that in Chicago as Chi. is where Joe E. got his start but that was just an error on my part and tho't they would of forgot the story by this late date. So anyway these gorills come and ask me to work for them in this new room they have, it being in the Loop dist. So being idle at the time I gave my consent before either one of us had time to change our mind. They tell me to come around Thurs. and I do.

How is the story.

Who is the mouse in the story.

Therefore we have where, how and who.

So I am rehearsing and they have a line consisting of six mice and only one of them you wd take to a building excavaton, or else take all six of them there and throw five of them in where it is deepest. It is the kind of a line where they all do challenge dances to make it look like they were all good hoofers or anyway make it seem like they had a line of 16 mice. The mobbers who run the joint have a relapse and decided to spend a small sum on advertising and that is how this Melba comes into my life. Melba works on one of these Chi. papers and there is very little doing in the clubs in the summer and so when the papers get a buck from club ads they like to play ball. So they decide to give us a little free publicity and send Melba around to get an interview with nobody else but yr. pal Joey. It is for the Sunday paper.

Well we are rehearsing and I am doing a patter with the kids in the line where they come up to me one by one and ask me what I want for Xmas and it is all the double entender. But it is the way I play it that is funny. I do not know exactly who to compare myself with but for illustraton Maurice Chevalier. I am having trouble with one of the mice because she is mugging even in rehearsal and as far as I could make out is doing her impresson of Kate Hepburn and any minute will go into her impresson of L. Barrymore. A poor man's Shiela Barret. In there punching and trying to crab *my* act. So I gave up in disgust and went over and sat down till Duilio, the boss came over and asked me why and I said I was all in favor of giving a fugitive from Maj. Bowes a little helpful push but wd be God damned if I wd play straight for them when it is my own act. I said you people have gone out and spent money advertising that I was going to open as master of ceremonies and then some mouse getting $23 a wk comes along and you might as well not have me there as it is a waste of money. Get her to get her brother or old man free, I said and you won't have to pay me. Duillo agreed and said "Well I guess you are tired and why don't you take 15 minutes and during that time I will tell

her" and so I sat down and was having a quiet
powder when in came something. I was tired
and only raised my eyes when she came in but
I tho't to myself Lesbo. I looked at her and tho't
well so this is the kind of a joint I picked and
did not know it. I tho't I could peg a joint like
that from 2 mi. away and always did before but
here I tho't I am all set to be m. c. in a crib
where the Lesbos even come and watch the
dress rehearsals. I am trying to give you the first
impresson of this something. She is wearing this
suit that you or I wd turn down because of
being too masculine. Her hair is cut crew cut
like the college blood. She is got on a pair of
shoes without any heels and a pr. of glasses that
make her look like she lost something but gave
up the hope that she will ever find it. Then
standing behind her is a little fat guy and when
I first saw him I tho't now what the hell do
those two do together. Then I got another look
when she moved towards me and I saw he had
a camera and I almost bursted out laughing.
"They are going to make some postcards for
their private collecton," I tho't. Then the dame
came closer to me and I was just about to cover
my face with my hands and scream but then
Duilio came over and said hello to her and
shook hands and you wd think she was Mrs.
Marshall Fields the way he bowed and cowtow
to her. "What is this?" I said to myself, because

Duilio is not double gaited as far as I knew but before I had a chance to do any more thinking he came over and introduced her to me and she gave me a slight brush and said okay let's sit over here and talk and she only had about a half an hour she said. Then Duilio menton that Miss so and so was the one that ran the night club dep't on some paper and gave me a punch in the ribs to con her into a good story.

Well she sat down and she ordered a double Scotch and water on the side and started out saying "What is a nice boy like you doing in a place like this?" Oh, a wise guy, I tho't. So I tho't I wd be a wise guy with her so I said it was okay if she wanted to look down on my job but I said some people have too much pride to go on relief and since I was able to entertain people with a few songs and stories I wd rather do that in preference to being just a bum. Oh, she said, you have pride and I said I was born with it. I said I had to quit college because the family lost our fortune and she wanted to know what college and I told her Dartmouth University. There I made a mistake. She said you never went to any Dartmouth and I said I ought to know and she said yes you ought to know they call it Dartmouth College and not Dartmouth u. I said when I was there we preferred to call it Dartmouth u. and she said yes, when you were there it probably was a university but you were never there yet. So she said let it pass and tell me about that family fortune that the family lost. Was it well up in 3 figures? I said I was not brought up to boast about the am't of how much we had but if she wanted to know something when daddy blew his brains out in 1929 all the papers called him the millionaire sportsman and very sarcastically I said and of course the papers are always right. I said what did I know about how much he use to have? All I know was he left mother penniless. Sad, she said. Very sad. I said no not any more because mother was contented on the few pittances I was able to provide her and did not care any more about our fortune. I said may I ask where she went to college and she said she went to Mount Holy Oak. I said see the diff. bet. you and I. I said you bring up a place that I never heard of but I did not go ahead and deny there was any such place. I said the country is full of these small Catholic girls schools like Mount Holy Oak and I only had the greatest respect for them being a Catholic myself on mother's side. Okay, she said.

I thought I made my impression by putting her in her place but the more the fool I. I wasnt satisfied with the crap I handed her but had to put it on thicker and all this time she stopped asking me questions but just listened, me thinking she was taking it all in and that I had her spellbounded with my stories about polo and yacting and our huge estate. Then all of a sudden she held up her hand like a traffic cop and said you can stop now before you run down. It is been fascinating and thank you but she did not have time for any more. I said what did she mean and she said "Pally I never heard so much crap in such a short time in my life. Such a fertle imaginaton it is a pity to be wasted in a nite club. I will write my own story but it wont be as good as yrs." Okay Moe, she said to the fat little camera man and he came over and then she called one of the mice and said something to her and the two of them went to the dressing room and about 5 min. later she came back but I did not know her. What she did was undergo a complete transformaton and took off her cloths and got into panties and brasserie that belong to one of the mice and took off her glasses and for the 1st time in many wks I forgot about Lana Turner. Yes that is how good this Melba was. Gams and a pair of maracas that will haunt me in my dreams and what is more when she got makeup on she was even pretty. I did not get the point but she said come on (to me) and put her arm in mine and posed like she was doing some kind of a dance step with me. She said Girl reporter at nite club rehearsal with the new m. c. sensaton. Girl reporter lives life of nite club entertainers. She had me all over the place smiling and posing like we were dancing together. She said it was all pictures for the Sunday paper. Well I was a willing subject because anything to get my hands on her. All the time Moe kept taking pictures. Then she stopped and went back and got into her rags and by the time she was dressed and shoed and glassed again I recovered my composer. To think of this going around Chicago and never anybody knowing about it because of the disguise. I said I hope she wd come to the opening but she said she wd not be found dead in a nite club and got over that yrs ago so I said well I did not blame her because it was a shallow life &c. and said I wd like to talk to her some time about it and she burst out laughing and said dont waste yr time. You just got a little bit of a shock I am aware but you just saw as much as you will ever see so get rid of such ideas because among other things my husband use to play football at Dartmouth U. as you call it. He is also satisfactory in every other way and I must be running along. It's been nice knowing you &c. So how do you like that? It is like the primative savages that make their women wear viels right here in the 2d biggest city in the country. But I learned one thing to never judge a book by its cover and the only trouble is when I walk along the street I am always passing up the pretty mice and going on the make for the tired ones dressed like girl scout masters.

PAL JOEY

Reminiss?

FRIEND TED:

I was only thinking the other day how it is every once in a while I get home late at nite and as the old no. use to have it I climb the stair and nobody is there but me and my shadow and how because of our kind of an occupaton it is too late to call anybody but something for a fin or a duece who will come up and entertain you. But not good enough. I guess what you do you stand there leading one of the Naton's No. 1 name Bands all nite and see Betty there all nite and wd. not apprisiate any but the best and the same with me. Here I am in Chi and some nice mice are in Chi and know a lot of the best and wd. not be contented with any but the best. That is what happens to the both of us. I give with the vocals and wolf around in a nite club and see the best and it is not good enough if I can call up the highest paid bag in Chi and get it for $^{1}/_{2}$. Mostly at that time of the nite I want it for free and with love too at that.

Thence I look around my tiny nook of an apt.

and see how I have a buck here & there hid in under the rug or a doz. Charvette ties from some souvenier of a romantic ideal. But feel sorry for my self all the same except when I happened to think I am also a man with a few good friends in this world and of them all there is none more highly prized than you Ted. Yes, I mean it. Some have the opinion that Joey, yr old pal Joey is a chap that if he did not have another breath of the body it wd be okay with them and they may be right. All of my life I did things that I wished I did not do because of hurting people like in Cincinatti that time we ganged that poor unfortunate mouse that you and I and also Kell went around with it in a sling for the best part of a yr. I recall that very distinctly because of still getting bills from that quack in Pittsburg and if I were you Ted wd pay that little tab as he is getting nasty with me but you have a Name Band. Also the time when that lug in Pa. coal regons was trying to pay us off in the dark and was it you slugged him or me and we got in the bus and were in Maryland before he opened up his eyes. I wished I could reminiss about the time at the Penn State College which was some Prom and we took $50 off some College boy that wanted to have some summer job and we said we wd fix him with Waring. Well we had some great old times together you & I and I guess that is why when I get home some nites alone and wd. rather sit down and write to my friend Ted than waste my time on the phone winning some high paid bageroo.

That is exactly how the situaton is tonite and am sitting here and wish we had a jug of that corn stuff they gave us at the Virgina University and could talk it over and reminiss. I guess one time when we had a lot of fun was the time when we had the Battle of Music vs a college band the Barbury Coast Band from Dartmouth U. They said they were from Barbury Coast because of some reason I forget. But from Dartmouth U. I guess that was pretty nearly the 1st time I moved in on a society deb down at Webster Hall in the village but it burn down. I seem to have recalled that we made the college boys play all nite or any way 2 hrs straight meanwhile you and I and Pete and Noodles and Chick moved in on the society debs. We were all kids then and tho't how it was tough to move in on a society deb and I guess we tho't we wd all end up with a Jordan roadster in those days. I said I was from Princeton. I remember that much. I did not even know if Princeton was in Phila.

Well friendship is a great thing especially in our occupaton where we never get home at a decent hr. I seem to have recall that one time we were booked in the old Ballaban & Katz Publix or I guess you were not along that time

but it was just after you went with Goldkette
and I went along with the band and Sparky
Bosch took his wife along for some un-known
reason that I will never be able to understand.
Mike Shortridge was suppose to be ahead of
the band then but doubling back and our best
interest at heart till one nite we played the 1st
show and went out and it was this town Chi.
where I now am and we went out to pollute the
lungs with fresh air and the shock of it or something he ate put Sparky right on the pavement,
out like a light. They had to get somebody to
take him home as we were on again in 5 mins.
But by the time he got back to the flea bag
where we were staying he felt okay but did not
feel so okay when he went up to his room and
discovered that Mike Shortridge and his little 2
wks old bride were in the kip and did not want
to be interrupted by Sparky or any body else. I
am sorry you missed that as Mike was around
50 yrs of age and Sparky around 21 but Sparky
was always a fresh punk and Mike use to be a
football star at Georga Teck. Sparky played a lot
of horn in his day but he never got a lip like he
got from Mike. Mike is a kind of a guy that you
dont interrupt him when he is in the kip with
a little 2 wks old bride even if it is yr bride.

Do you ever think about the old days? I do. I
read the thing in the *Down Beat* about you
about how at 30 you are still an old timer but

maybe they meant two timer or double timer or back timer (only kidding Ted). I give them the same thing myself only they do not ask me. I mean *Down Beat* does not ask me. But in Chi. they do not recall I was here when Isham was still here at the College Inn. I even wear a little little rug up front but so does the Grooner and Freddie Astare. I can level with them and tell them I do not know what they mean by the Loop because I wd rather forget most of the times I was here before. Jack Jenney and Carl Kress and Manny Klein go right thru town and never give me a bell and I guess they think they are hot stuff by so doing. But if you want to know the truth I wish they wd never look me up or give me a bell as the Chi people are of the opinon I am a kid from the Princeton college and if they see me around with Klein and Kress and Jenney and like Freeman and them these Chi. people know a lot about band guys and wd wonder how I knew them so well. I cultivated young Bobby Hackett so as I wd look younger when Hacket went thru here with Horace Heidt. Christ I knew Bix. I read all this stuff about Bix and how wonderful he was and all I remember about Bix was the article I saw in the Life mag. where Bud said he did not wash his feet. Well I never saw Hackett with his shoes off but for my dough he is a bare footed coal miner if that is the way Bix got to play good cornet.

Friend Ted I was just thinking of a bad wk in Pa. every summer for a couple summers. Do you remember Lakewood, Lakeside, Berwick, Schulkill Park, Reading, Mealey's in Allentown, Bach's in Reading, the Island nr. Harrisburg, Maher's in Shenadoh, Rocky Glen nr. Scranton and Manila Grove near Tamaqua? Boy I could go on with them and so could you. I wish we had a chance to reminiss some nite even tho you are the leader of the Naton's No. 1 band. Not that I am not doing okay in Chi. because I am. I often think to myself that what if I turned out to be a Channcey Morehouse and a Dave Tough? That wd mean I was a really good drummer but not the lug that does not know a flammadiddle from a high hat. I put on such a good act here in Chi. that I kid myself and think I do not remember how to play Jazz Me. Jack Gallagher could sing it good and he only had one arm. I have both my arms so there is not any reason why I never sang it as equally as good. Do you recall the look of a surprise on Frank Trumbaur's kisser the nite I picked up an E flat alto and gave a slight job on Farewell Blues and he did not know I could play sax but also did not know that was the only thing I could play and the wart stood out as if he wanted to stab me with it. I ruined the reed that nite but always did not when I picked up an E flat alto but when I put it down. I guess this coun-

try is full of sax players that b't new reeds on
acc't of me playing one chorus of Farewell
Blues. Well you take a sax player and I will take
a left handed pitcher. Put them all together they
spell dixie.

Methinks I will not turn this missile over to the
Post as it is just reminissing from here to
Atlantic City but I had a lot of fun out of it
writing a letter to my friend Ted without
putting the arm on him for a couple of bucks.
Ted the only all around honest decent guy I
ever knew except for one or two instants that
if some mouse was not mixed up in it wd not
of happened. Ted you are a great guy and should
of been a priest the way yr mother said. Ted old
friend am waiting for a bageroo for free and
could go on writing to you and reminissing
from here to Atlantic City Steel Pier 10 wks
guaranteed but methinks the bageroo is got
her finger wedged in my doorbell. Will leave
her wait a minute or two and teach her a good
lesson not to get her fing. wedged in a gentle-
man's door bell at this hour of the night. If it is
the one I called up she wd not miss a finger
because she lost everything else when the boys
came back with Gen. Dewey in the Span.
American War.

Ted old friend how the hell are you and how
does it feel to be rich?

Will bet you put yr dough into an insurance

innuity and send the rest home to yr mother. I
never saw you even pick up a tab for 4 mocha
java coffees you cheap larceny jerk if there ever
was one. I know you gave me the X X or otherwise I wd be making those so called wise
cracks with Robins Burns every Thurs. and wd
have my own stable of horses. It is a good thing
I only write you letters instead of getting a
hinge at yr holy kisser so I could hang a bloop-
er on it. Friend Ted I am speaking to you and
will tear this up but always was

Yr
EX PAL JOEY
(Hate yr guts)

BUTTERFIELD 8

John O'Hara

with a new introduction by MATTHEW J BRUCCOLI

"a great social realist" VILLAGE VOICE

Set amid Manhattan's fast set in the early 1930s,
Butterfield 8 is the tale of a sexual encounter
between a married society man and a tragically
corrupted young woman that tears both their
worlds apart. Told from a number of perspectives, it
shows Manhattan in a state of turmoil – a society
where the Crash and Prohibition have left the old
certainties in tatters, vividly capturing the beautiful
and damned of the speakeasy crowd. It is one of
the finest works by one of the greatest American
novelists of the century.

Butterfield 8 was filmed in 1960, starring Laurence
Harvey, Eddie Fisher and Elizabeth Taylor in an
Oscar-winning role as Gloria.

1-85375-319-X
£5.99